GHOSTFIELD

MICHAEL YOWELL

World Castle Publishing, LLC
Pensacola, Florida
Copyright © Michael Yowell 2022
Paperback ISBN: 9781956788808
eBook ISBN: 9781956788815
First Edition World Castle Publishing, LLC, April 18, 2022
http://www.worldcastlepublishing.com
Licensing Notes
Cover: Karen Fuller
Editor: Maxine Bringenberg

PART I

CHAPTER 1
ROAD TRIP

"I can't fucking believe we're doing this."

Everybody in the car delivered stunned looks to Jim. The only sound heard in the sudden quiet was the humming of the CR-V's tires on the highway.

"What?" the young man said, defensively. "I mean, come on…this isn't exactly a typical weekend getaway."

Lance Bowser removed one hand from the steering wheel and raised a skinny finger. "True. But it's gonna be *so* fucking cool."

"Ghost lights…." Jim's voice was skeptical but not quite disapproving. "Shit, Bowser. Whatever made you even *look* for something like that?"

Lance shrugged his thin shoulders. "I dunno. Just a result of drinking and web surfing."

Jim Laverdure leaned back, placing his hands behind his long, black hair. "Ah yes. I know a thing or two about that. One of my Indian names is 'Drinks With Internet-Porn.'"

He often joked about whatever "Indian name" suited the moment, which he could get away with because his bloodline was of the Zuni tribe.

Karen and David, also sitting in the back with Jim, chuckled heartily. Their laughter incited Jim to keep going.

"But right now, my name is 'Pisses Like Racehorse.' Find a place to stop, will ya, Bowser? Otherwise, we'll all be called 'Swims Inside Honda.'"

Jaelyn buried her face in her hands to hide her giggling, and her long, brown hair bounced atop her chest. The statement also spoke for her, however, and she addressed Lance. "Yeah, I gotta go too. I think stopping's a good idea."

Lance nodded. It had been a while since their last pit stop, and he would also feel better after a bathroom visit. His irritable bowel syndrome made road trips a challenge; he never knew when his body was going to suddenly feel the need for a bowel movement. He learned to keep it at bay by trying to go every time an opportunity to use a restroom presented itself. It was a humbling feeling, one he had been dealing with ever since he left home two years ago to start attending college. But he would not let his condition stop him from doing things with his friends—as long as there were restrooms along the way.

They had been on the road for over ten hours. Their journey began early in the morning at the Arizona State campus, took them northeast through mountain and desert terrains, and had now brought them to the Colorado border. Aside from bathroom breaks, gas fill-ups, and their lunch stop in Albuquerque, they were making good travel time.

Lance spotted a truck stop sign at the exit ahead. He

took the off ramp, pulled in, and parked the Honda at the gas pumps. His four passengers walked inside to find the restrooms while Lance filled the gas tank. Then Lance went inside to use the toilet before resuming the journey.

Once all five were back in the CR-V, Lance started the engine and drove them back to the highway. Gazing at the familiar Colorado landscape ahead, he smiled. It was nice to be back in his home state.

David Lucero had grown up with Lance in the foothills city of Pueblo. They had been best friends since junior high, and now the young Latino was Lance's off-campus roommate. They were both studying journalism and were in several classes together.

Jaelyn Graham also shared a class with Lance. At first, she had ignored the lanky student; he was not a fraternity man. He was very average looking, tall and skinny, with dark-brown hair parted neatly on the left. But after a while, she grew fond of his wit, personality, and intellect. Her sorority sisters even approved of him when the two started dating each other.

Especially Karen Stanton. Having warded off the advances of a multitude of prickly frat boys, she appreciated how sweet and genuine Lance was. "He's a keeper," she had told Jaelyn after first meeting him.

Rounding off the group was Jim Laverdure. The next-door neighbor to Lance and David, Jim was quite a character. He had introduced himself to them as "Indian Jim," an unexpected icebreaker that showed his lighthearted side. Despite his daunting Native American jawline and piercing eyes, he was a hilarious, harmless, lovable young man. Jim was the class clown, the life of the party, the fun friend. He was proud of his Zuni heritage but liked to have fun with it when among friends.

It was a good group of comrades with good chemistry. They each seemed to enjoy the company of the others. They were always finding ways to have a great time together. And now, before starting their junior year, they were taking their last adventure of the summer.

"Okay, so how much farther?" asked Jaelyn, feeling weary.

"I think we're about two hours away."

"Thank God," said Karen. "I'm gonna need a drink after this long trip."

"It'll be worth it," Lance assured. At least he hoped it would be.

"So, remind me why we thought this long-ass drive was a good idea?" said Jim.

David, who had initially suggested this excursion, chimed in. "Dude, this is *ghosts*. And not the fake shit you see on those ghost-hunting shows. This is the real deal. You'll actually be able to *see* them."

"That would be cool," Jim admitted, "but I'm not holding my breath. I'll believe it when I see it."

"Have faith, my friend," said David. "Everything I've read about this place makes me convinced we're going to see something."

"You said this was an old Western mining town we're going to?" asked Karen.

"Silver Valley. A small town in the middle of the mountains."

"So, these are, like, ghosts of dead cowboys and miners?"

"Yep," David and Lance said in unison.

"And maybe Indians," added Jaelyn.

"My kind of people," said Jim. "I mean the 'Indian' part, not the 'dead' part."

David elaborated more on what they were to expect. "There's a church on the edge of town, with a graveyard. That's where people can see ghost lights floating at night. They just dance around, all different sizes and colors."

"The people or the lights?" Jim asked, cracking himself up.

"The lights, dumb-ass," giggled David, scratching his short, spiked hair. "And they can best be seen on the darkest nights. That's why we picked this weekend to do this. New moon."

The students continued conversing and cajoling while they journeyed along the highway. The scenery gradually changed from desert sage and tumbleweeds to colorful, rocky foothills to looming mountains. They were soon driving west up a two-lane mountain highway that cut through the thick pine forest.

Lance admired the scenery along the way. A tumbling river ran alongside the highway, sandwiched by granite cliffs and steep, lush hillsides. Although he grew up in Colorado, Lance had never been through this region of the mountains. It was awe-inspiring. The beauty all around them further affirmed his recently-discovered faith in a divine creator.

Eventually, they weaved their way down the other side of the range to emerge into a broad valley. About ten miles wide, the flat field separated two mountain ranges. In the middle of the plain, a small town was visible.

"There it is," said David, confirming his statement by checking the locator on his phone. "We're here."

"Finally," Karen moaned thankfully, rolling her pretty, light-blue eyes.

David looked at her and smiled. He was captivated by Karen. When he had heard Jaelyn's sorority sister wanted to accompany them on this journey, he was delighted. He could never get enough of the cute blonde's mesmerizing eyes. They were like aquamarine gems glimmering in the sun.

"Hey look, there's the graveyard!" Lance announced, and everybody followed his finger.

On the outskirts of the town ahead, an old church sat off to the left. A sizable cemetery could be seen farther to the left and then the barren fields.

"Pull over," said Jaelyn. "I want to get a picture."

"Good idea," Lance replied. He found a wide spot on the shoulder and stopped the car there. Then he shut off the engine, and everybody stepped out of the CR-V.

The town of Silver Valley lay out before them. The remote community consisted of about two dozen interwoven streets containing houses and small buildings. To the right of town, a few abandoned mines were visible. The rustic setting was picture worthy, and Jaelyn made sure to capture all of it.

The rest of the group took pictures as well. This was a sight they might never see again, and they wanted to capture the memory. A few shots were taken of the distant town, but most of their attention was drawn to the focus of their journey — the cemetery.

They had to zoom in to see the tombstones. All in all, there appeared to be hundreds. *An awful lot of dead people for such a small town*, Lance noted. Then his eye caught some grave markers out in the field past the cemetery. *Even more out there.*

He turned to check on the rest of the group. They appeared to be finished with their picture taking. "Good?" he asked, and the others nodded.

Lance looked out at the field one last time. A breeze tickled the back of his neck, and he shuddered slightly. Then he brought everyone back inside the Honda, started the engine, and drove toward town.

CHAPTER 2
CHECKING IN

"What do you mean you didn't book a hotel?"

David shrugged. "Don't need to. It's a small town in the middle of nowhere; I'm sure there're vacancies everywhere."

Lance shook his head. "Except for other people like us that come to town to see the ghost lights."

"Are you kidding? Nobody hears about these ghost lights. *You* never heard about them until you accidentally found them on the internet."

"Dude, you better be right. I don't intend on spending the next two nights in the car."

"We'll be fine." David began searching for hotels on his cell phone.

While his friend looked for lodging, Lance continued driving. The group had just arrived on Main Street and was beginning their tour through town. The two-lane streets were adorned with old shops, bars, and small restaurants.

"Man," said Jim, "this really is a small town."

"Yeah," Lance replied. "Only about three hundred if you saw that population sign on the way in."

"We'd better find a hotel here."

"Chill out, Jim," said David. "Here's one," he then announced, holding up his phone. "The Silver Inn. Looks like it's at the far edge of town up ahead."

"Thank God," mumbled Karen, who was longing for the day's journey to end. The rest of the group was equally ready to be out of the car. It was time to get their fun and exciting weekend started.

David guided Lance to the motel he had found, and they pulled into the parking lot three minutes later. Everybody spilled out of the car and strolled to the lobby entrance. They approached the front desk and were greeted by a friendly clerk.

"How're you all doing today?" the young man beamed.

"Good," said Lance. "We need some rooms."

The employee's smile melted into a frown. "Oooh, I'm afraid we don't have any."

Lance was not sure he had heard correctly. "What? You have no rooms?"

"No, sorry. All booked up. There's a big wedding party here this weekend."

"Here?" scoffed Jim. "I mean, no offense, but...*here?*"

"Sorry," the young man repeated. "You might try the Travel Stop down 5th Street."

"Okay, thanks anyway." Lance turned to address his friends. "Travel Stop it is."

"On it," said David. He began typing into his phone while the band of disappointed students vacated the lobby and returned to the parking lot.

They boarded the CR-V, and Lance started it up. He noticed there were about fifteen cars in the parking lot, which validated the clerk's statement about all the rooms being booked. With a sigh, he pulled away and drove slowly to give his roommate time to find their next destination.

"Okay," David informed, "I've got the Travel Stop. Take your next right, then go to 5th and hang left."

Lance drove them to their next option. Spotting the motel, he pulled into the parking lot. The crew stepped out and walked to the front door.

A middle-aged woman with short, red hair was working the desk. She acknowledged the group with a pleasant smile. "Howdy, folks," she greeted.

"Hello," said Lance. "Do you have a couple of rooms available?"

"Sorry, afraid not. We're all full up. Usually, we're never full, but this weekend —"

"Let me guess," said Jim. "A big wedding?"

The woman nodded. "Yeah, families that came in from Colorado Springs."

Jim eyed David ominously. "Strike two."

"Any other hotels in town we can try?" Lance asked the clerk. "We've already been to the Silver Inn, and they were full too."

"Only other place you could try would be Sally's. She runs a little bed and breakfast a couple blocks away. Just head straight that way until you see the bright green house, can't miss it."

"Okay, thank you," said Lance. Then he and his friends

left, their spirits deflated.

Filing back into the vehicle, everybody sighed. "All right, I guess we try the bed and breakfast," said Karen.

"It'll cost more," Lance frowned, "but if that's all we've got...." He started the motor and drove his friends down the street to the bed and breakfast. They spotted the bright green house immediately.

The group waited in the Honda while Lance trudged up the steps to the front door, knocked, and disappeared inside. It took less than a minute for Lance to come back out, shaking his head as he walked back to the car.

Lance returned to the driver seat, his eyes locked on David. "Well," he reported, "no luck here either." The group groaned in dismay.

"Fuuuuck," whined Jim. "Way to go, David."

The Latino's hands flew up in the air. "How the hell was I supposed to know somebody was gonna have their crazy-big wedding up here? I mean, come on! What was I supposed to expect?"

"To have to book rooms, 'Sleeps In Ditch.'"

"And why was that my responsibility anyway? Any of you could've booked rooms just as easily."

"True," Lance admitted. "I guess we just assumed that since you planned the trip, the dates, etcetera, that you'd taken care of the hotel."

"Come on, guys," said Jaelyn. "There has to be another hotel. Even if it's in the next county over."

Lance nodded. "You're right. We'll find rooms somewhere."

"See?" said David, jokingly. "That's exactly what I

thought."

"Less talk-ie, more find-ie, amigo," Jim nagged.

"On it, ya grumpy Indian," confirmed David. He resubmitted the search, widened the search zone, and scanned the results the phone produced on its map.

While David continued to look for lodging, Lance drove slowly through the town. He soon found himself on the outer corner of town, with the two-lane highway not far beyond that.

"Hey, look over there," said Jaelyn, and the others did so. They saw what clearly looked like a motel just ahead on the right. As the car drew nearer, the crew could see a sign on the second-story railing that read: THE VALLEY INN.

"What do you know?" Lance muttered. "No one mentioned *this* one to us. And the parking lot is practically empty."

"All right," said Jim. "That's what I'm talking about."

"Fuckin' A," David smiled, feeling that the pressure on him was now going to disappear. "Let's go get some rooms!"

Lance steered into the lot and parked. The crew jumped out of the vehicle and found the entrance to the office.

An older man stood behind the desk, smoke from his cigarette swirling around the ashtray behind him. He looked to be about fifty or so, with salt-and-pepper hair combed across the top of his head. He pressed his horn-rimmed glasses tighter to his face and waved at the visitors.

"Howya awl doin'?" he said. The man had a distinct Cajun accent, which took the group by surprise; it was not what they expected to hear coming from someone who resided in the Rocky Mountains.

"Good," Lance replied. "We need a couple of rooms. Do you have any vacancies?"

The man nodded nonchalantly. "Quite a few, actually. Single rooms are fiddy a night, or you can take da suite for seventy-five."

Lance raised his eyebrows, intrigued. "A suite, eh?" He looked over to his friends with enthusiasm.

"Well," the man confirmed, "it's what you might call a suite—has two beds and a couch. Plus a kitchenette widda full-size fridge."

David did the math. "That would work. Two in each bed, one on the couch."

"No, no," said Karen, not wanting them all to be crammed into one room. "How about me and Jaelyn getting our *own* room, and you three guys do what you want?" She looked at her sorority sister. "Don'tcha think?"

Jaelyn agreed. "I do."

David shrugged innocently. "Whatever. We'll take the suite. That way, we can all at least hang out in there until we're ready to crash. The kitchenette will come in handy."

"That it will," seconded Jim. The beer in their cooler was not going to stay cold too much longer.

"Okay," said Lance. "We'll take one room and the suite. Two nights."

"Yessir," the man confirmed, reaching for keys on the wall behind him. "One room and one suite." He produced a form for the young guests to fill in. "Just write yo' info here, initial here and here, and sign for me at da bottom."

Lance took a pen from the counter and began to write. "So, where are you from, if you don't mind my asking?"

"Ah, my Western accent didn't fool ya?" the man said sarcastically. He cackled at his own comment. "Me and da wife come from Louisiana, many years ago. Decided it would be a brilliant idea to buy us a motel here in da middle'a nowhere." He leaned closer. "So, da lesson is: stay in school, kids."

The guests laughed. "I like him," stated Karen. "He's awesome."

"Agreed," said Lance. Then he faced the owner. "So, we've been searching all over town for a hotel that had vacancies. It was sheer luck that we found you while driving by. Why is it nobody around here told us about you?"

The man scratched behind his ear. "I ain't too pop'lar 'round here. Da town don't like outsiders."

"Yet they don't mind filling their hotels," Jim noted.

"Oh, sure. Love tourists, yes. People who *live* here who ain't from here, not so much. Even when my wife died, didn't hear much from 'em."

"That's awful," said Jaelyn. "I'm so sorry to hear that."

The owner shrugged. "Is what it is. On a different note, what is it brought y'awl up here this weekend? Da weddin'?"

David grinned. "We're here for the ghost lights."

"Ah, yes. People go gaga for da ghost lights." He did not sound enthusiastic.

Lance picked up on the man's indifference. "Sounds like you're not too crazy about them. Have you ever seen them?"

"No, can't say that's somethin' I care to see. How did y'awl hear about 'em?"

"The Internet," said Lance.

"Ah yes. Damn Internet. Stirs up things that weren't

meant to be found."

Karen was beginning to have second thoughts about their upcoming excursion to the cemetery. "What do you mean?" she probed.

"I'll tell you da same thing I tell da others. If you're going for da ghost lights, stay in da cemetery. Beyond that is da fields, which is private property." He leaned in. "And folk around here shoot trespassers."

"Who lives there?" asked Jim. Then, after receiving a *why-the-hell-would-that-matter* look from everybody, he added, "Maybe we could go ask them for permission to go on their land."

The motel owner shook his head. "No, son. Da Amish live out there. And they keep to their own. Just trust me, stay off their land."

"We will," Lance assured. "And thanks for the info."

The group was assigned their rooms, and the owner took credit cards from David and Jaelyn in order to split the payment. Then, after thanking the owner, they left the office to grab their gear and lug it to their rooms on the second floor.

The girls found their room adequate. It had two queen-size beds and a bathroom, which was all they would need. Most of their time would be spent out around town and hanging out with the boys in the suite.

The suite was what the owner had described. A kitchenette containing a refrigerator, cooktop, and microwave, a small couch, a decent table with four chairs, a TV mounted on the wall, and two queen-size beds. The students hauled their belongings inside and set them on the dingy, orange carpet.

"Awesome," said Jim, nodding at the table. "We can play drinking games."

"Speaking of which," David noted, "we should get the beer out of the cooler and into the fridge." He went to the refrigerator, made sure it was on, and reached back for the fiberglass cooler that was brought closer by the others.

"Okay," Jim said, handing a beer to each of his friends. "Let's pop one open to celebrate finally getting here."

"Amen," said Karen. The group opened their beer cans and began to drink. "Then after this," she added, "we should probably find a place to eat dinner."

Lance nodded. "Yeah. And maybe a quick drive to the graveyard first, to find the best way there while it's still light out."

David agreed. "Yep, that way, we'll have no trouble finding it tonight." He took a deep swig. "This is gonna be so fucking awesome, you guys!"

Jim raised his beer and said, "*Banzai!*"

Lance offered his usual response. "*Kanpai!*"

The group drank their beers to loosen up for the evening ahead of them.

CHAPTER 3
DINNER CONVERSATION

The summer sun was drifting low in the sky. It would start to get dark in another hour or so. The crew climbed into the Honda, and Lance drove them out of the motel parking lot.

They took note of a few restaurants and taverns while traveling Main Street. One looked like an Italian eatery, and the group decided they would go there to eat. But first, a quick excursion to the cemetery would be carried out, so they would know the route later that night.

David pulled up the area's map on his phone. "Found it. Follow this road around to the right, then take your last left. That'll take us straight out to the church."

"Cool," said Lance. He drove along the town's perimeter until they saw the dirt road leading to the church. He turned onto the road, and the group saw the small church a few hundred yards ahead of them. Before the church, on their right, was a neglected baseball field, and they could see a few Amish boys pitching, hitting, and catching there.

"Look, how cute!" Jaelyn remarked. Observing the boys was like watching an old movie about times past. The young Amish were wearing their home-sewn white shirts and suspenders, having simple fun while their horse and buggy were tied up nearby. "They look just like I would've imagined."

Lance smiled at the sight. "Yep." He drove slowly past, watching the youngsters. The boys did not even acknowledge the passersby.

David studied the map. "This road keeps going past the graveyard, but it stops about half a mile out."

"That's probably where the Amish land begins," said Lance. He brought them to the church and parked on the side of the road. The group got out for a quick inspection of the area.

The church was meager in size, only about fifteen feet wide and thirty feet long, with a small steeple perched atop the front end. It looked like something built during the town's inception, the sagging roof and bowing stoop showing its age. But it had been kept up for the most part. Bright white paint covered the wooden exterior evenly. And there was a shiny padlock on the door, indicating the church was still being attended to.

The crew walked around the side of the church and to the cemetery behind it. They viewed what appeared to be hundreds of headstones and grave markers, all packed tightly together inside the wire-fenced graveyard.

In the distance, across the valley, the group could see an Amish farm. "Man," said David, "they do live quite a ways away from town."

"They like their privacy," Lance stated. "They have their own little world."

The sun was beginning to sink behind the mountains west of town. Having found their way to the cemetery, they could now go back into town to eat dinner. Lance drove the crew back to the Italian restaurant they had decided to try.

When they entered the restaurant, rich aromas of sausage, garlic, tomato sauce, oregano, and baked cheeses enticed them. The smells brought both comfort and hunger to the young students. Noticing a sign that instructed guests to seat themselves, the group made their way inside to a large table in the corner. They sat, admiring the dimly-lit room decorated with black-and-white photographs of Italian celebrities.

A waitress with long, curly, blonde hair strolled over to take their orders. She was short, a tad pudgy, and fairly young; she looked to be not much older than the students.

"Hello," she greeted with a welcoming smile. "My name's Jeannette. What can I get you all to drink?"

"Hi, Jeannette," said Jaelyn. "Could I just start with a water? I'm parched."

"Sure, I'll bring waters out for everybody. Anyone want something else to drink?"

"Yeah," Jim nodded. "Can I get a Coke?"

David also requested a Coke, and the others were content with water for the time being. The waitress handed out menus, made some recommendations, and then left her guests to give them time to decide while she prepared their beverages.

"Ooh," said Karen, "the spinach ravioli sounds good."

"Barf," Jim remarked.

"Excuse me?" Karen said, incredulous.

"Rabbit food," the young man retorted. "You should eat something with *real* food in it, like meat, sausage."

She ran her fingers through her shoulder-length blonde hair and softened her eyes, messing with him. "So…you think I don't get any *sausage* in me?"

"Karen!" said Jaelyn, shocked but amused. She could not stifle her smile.

"What? Jim started it."

Jim raised his hands in front of him. "I was insinuating you were a *vege*tarian, not a *vagi*tarian."

Jaelyn's face turned to stone. "Ohmygod! *Jim!*"

The group laughed raucously but tried to contain the clamor to their table. After a moment, they all settled down and studied their menus. By the time the waitress returned with their drinks, they were ready to order.

Jeannette passed out the water glasses and two Cokes. "Here you go," she said with a warm grin. "You all sound like you're having a fun time. Where are you from?"

"ASU," said David. "The *capital* of fun."

"What brings you all the way up here?"

"We decided to come up this weekend to see the ghost lights."

The waitress's sparkle suddenly seemed to wane. "Oh," was all she said.

Lance sensed the change. "You don't sound too excited about them. Why's that?"

Jeannette shrugged. "Eh. When you've grown up here,

it's just not something you care about. That's all." She pulled a notepad from her apron. "So you all ready to order?"

The hungry crew ordered their meals and then watched the waitress scuttle away to the kitchen. Lance faced his roommate.

"Is it weird that nobody in this town thinks anything of the ghost lights?"

"A little," David concurred. "Makes you wonder."

"About whether this shit is real or not?" said Jim. "Or if we just wasted a really long time driving all the way up here?"

David rolled his eyes. "No, dickhead. I'm sure the ghost lights are a real thing." He was beginning to fear the worst— that he had convinced the others to come here for nothing— but he still trusted that they were going to witness everything they had read about online. "You'll see. I just don't get why nobody here seems to be enthusiastic about them."

"Maybe because it's a hoax."

"I don't think so," Lance declared. "Like we saw online, everybody who comes here swears what they see is legit."

Karen wanted to hear about them again. "How do they describe them again?"

Lance took a sip of water and sat up straighter, remembering the details his online research had discovered. "They're like the orbs you see in photographs. Except these glow with a bright light. They tend to dance around the graveyard. Kind of like fireflies, but way bigger. And they vary in size, color, and intensity."

"So they'll all be different?" Karen asked. "Like snowflakes?"

Lance nodded. "Or fingerprints. We should see a variety of cool colors dancing around in the dark."

"A western rave," said Jim. His friends began laughing at the image Jim's joke provided. He layered it on. "But without the ecstasy…although there may be some peyote lying around."

"Maybe some magic mushrooms," noted Jaelyn.

"There ya go!" Jim guffawed. "Now we got ourselves a rave!"

Before long, Jeannette delivered their dinners to the table. The students were famished after the long day of travel, and they eyed the meals with great anticipation. The food looked and smelled delicious. The group thanked their waitress and dug in.

Ten minutes later, Jeannette returned to check in on her diners. They indicated they were fine and that the food was great. The waitress smiled and refilled their water glasses.

"So, Jeannette," said Jim. "I gotta ask you something."

"Sure."

"The guy at the motel told us to stay out of the field beyond the graveyard. He says the Amish would shoot us if they caught us trespassing. But aren't the Amish supposed to be peaceful?"

"The Amish *are* a peaceful folk," stated Jeannette. "I don't even think they believe in guns. They're totally harmless. Very sweet, actually, when they come into town. At least the younger generation."

"Then why would the motel owner tell us that?" asked Karen, puzzled.

Jeannette paused a moment before answering. "The

reason people don't go into the field is because some believe that's where the *bad* souls are kept."

The group looked at each other tentatively, cynicism on their faces.

"You know, villains and murderers, too evil to have the honor of being buried on the church grounds."

"Seriously?" David scoffed. "Like…uh…ghost exile in the field?"

"Uh huh." The waitress leaned closer. "My grandfather told me an old legend that there's buried treasure out there somewhere, in the grave of a *particular* bad cowboy, Black Jack."

Lance raised his eyebrows with interest.

"Black Jack," Jim chortled. "Sounds like a mean pirate. Like, 'Aaarrrgh, stay away from me buried treasure, ye pesky natives!'"

Jeannette giggled a little and then composed herself. "It was just something we heard growing up, a long time ago. I remember the story saying something about a 'dead pit' and 'Black Jack's marker,' but that's the only things that stuck with me."

The crew eyed each other with excited inspiration.

"Now relax," she quickly added. "It's just an old story, something he probably made up to get my imagination going. As kids, we used to search the field all day, and of course we never found anything but the old graves."

"Well," said Jaelyn, "all we're gonna look for tonight is the ghost lights."

"Come with us," Jim suggested. "What time do you get off?"

The waitress shook her head. "Oh no, thank you, not me. You all have fun, though. And be careful." Then she walked away to tend to her other tables.

The group did not mind Jeannette's refusal; they were perfectly content with going out by themselves. They finished their dinners, paid for the meal, and left.

It was still a bit too early to head back to the cemetery, so they found a bar just down the sidewalk and went inside. A couple of pitchers of beer would keep them busy for a few hours while they waited for it to get dark enough outside.

CHAPTER 4
THE CEMETERY

It was around ten o'clock when the crew left the bar. After waiting for Lance to use the restroom to appease his irritable bowel, they hopped into the Honda and headed toward the cemetery.

Lance drove the route they had familiarized themselves with hours earlier. He followed the road on the edge of town, spotted the dirt road to the church, and turned off. The group soon saw the church windows reflecting the CR-V's headlights.

"Here we go," said Jaelyn, her voice bubbly with anticipation. "I'm so ready for this."

They parked the car on the edge of the road in front of the small church. Eager and excited, the crew exited the vehicle and inspected their surroundings.

It was completely dark, with no moon lighting the sky. This was what the students had planned for. They knew coming here during a new moon would maximize the visibility of any luminous spirit activity. The darker the sky, the better the ghost lights.

Lance opened the tailgate and retrieved his flashlight. Then he turned it on and aimed the beam at the church.

Jim started walking toward the old structure. "The church looks super creepy at night."

The others voiced their agreement. The light beam wandered up the steps, the sagging stoop, and finally, the steeple of the pallid church. The building stood before them like an old, silent sentinel.

"Come on," said Karen. "Let's go see some ghosts!"

The group navigated the grounds of the churchyard, making their way around to the cemetery behind. Lance illuminated the path before them to keep them safe from tripping or stumbling. When they arrived at the graveyard, they stopped and looked around.

"So, where do we look?" asked Jim.

Lance shrugged in the dark. "Supposedly, they float around the graves, but they could be anywhere. I guess you'll see 'em wherever you see 'em."

The students studied the darkness surrounding them. The only light in the air came from the houses and buildings in town. No dancing ghost lights revealed themselves. Jim was beginning to think his skeptical feelings would prove to be right.

"Lemme see the flashlight," said David, holding out his hand. "I wanna check out some of these old tombstones."

Lance surrendered the flashlight, and David began to explore the cemetery. Some of the headstones and grave markers were polished stone, some were weathered, carved wood. David found them all interesting, as well as some of the inscriptions on them.

Before long, he returned to his companions. They were disappointed, having still not spotted any floating lights. But the crew would not give up hope yet. After all, they had come a long way to be here.

After thirty minutes of not seeing anything, however, the group was becoming sour.

"This sucks," said Lance. "I wanted *soo* badly to see these ghost lights."

Karen pulled her phone from her back pocket. "I'm gonna take some graveyard pics. See if I can get some ghost orbs."

David nodded. "Cool." He knew exactly what she was talking about, having taken some pictures in graveyards and old hotels where the images of round, translucent orbs occasionally graced the photographs. Most people dismissed orb images as dust particles caught in the light, but David did not accept that. Some of the orbs he had captured were in daylight, where no camera flash would have been aimed at them. And some of his images showed too much detail within the spheres for them to be blurry dust particles. He truly believed they were floating spirits.

David grabbed his own phone and activated the camera app. "Hang on, I'll take some with you." Checking the settings to make sure the flash was on, he stepped closer to Karen. He was interested in catching orbs with the camera, but he was also interested in Karen. Taking pictures was a nice chance for them to do something together. "All right, let's do this."

The pair wandered about the graves, capturing random images of the cemetery. The flash bursts from their phones lit the headstones brightly. After five minutes of picture taking, they stopped to take a look at what they had.

"I got some good shots," David stated, studying the gallery on his phone.

"Me too," said Karen. "I think I got some orbs."

David squeezed next to her to look at her pictures. It was harder to tell on a small camera screen, but some of the images showed some transparent, fuzzy circles in the air. "Yeah," he said, "those might be good ones."

"Might be," Karen shrugged. "I'll have to see what the pictures look like when I can see them on the big computer screen. But for now," she added while turning her phone off, "my battery is getting low. I'm gonna power down for a while."

They joined the others at the far end of the graveyard. "Any luck?" Lance asked.

"I think so," David replied. "We'll see how they turn out. You guys?"

Lance shook his head. "Nope. Haven't seen anything yet." There was disappointment and frustration in his voice.

Jim found a grassy patch between graves and sat. "Well," he proposed, "let's cop a squat and chill out for a little bit longer, and if we don't see anything by then, we'll go back to the motel and drink."

The others were good with that plan. Lance would stay there all night if he had to—he wanted to see the ghost lights that badly—but he would do what the group wanted to. They sat down on the cool ground to relax for a spell.

It was extremely dark in the moonless night. Any moving lights would be easy to spot. The students sat still in the silent gloom, patiently waiting for a sighting.

Then they heard the sound of hooves approaching.

"Shh," Jaelyn whispered. "Listen, something's coming."

The group heard a horse slowly drawing nearer, its hooves thumping and clopping on the hardened earth, but could not see anything in the pitch black. As it got closer, they could also hear the creaky wheels of a carriage being pulled behind the unseen animal.

Awful late for a horse ride, thought Lance. *Why the hell would a horse and buggy be out here this late in the dark?*

The invisible traveler passed by, about ten feet from where the students were sitting. The horse was snorting loudly and licking its chops. Lance pictured large, wood-colored teeth and flappy lips on the animal. The traveler continued on toward the field.

"Who the hell was that?" said David.

"Probably just one of the Amish heading home," Jim offered. "After a late night of whatever."

"Not in the pitch dark!" said Jaelyn. "They would need a lantern or something to see their way!"

"Were they on that dirt road over there?" asked Karen.

"No," David said. "They were closer, like right here through the graveyard."

"Where's the flashlight?" Jim asked.

"I've got it," said David.

"Well, turn it on, dumbass!" Jim directed. "I wanna see what just rode by us!"

"Okay, okay." The Latino stood up and aimed the flashlight in the direction of the passing horse. But the beam of bright light showed nothing but an empty graveyard. "What the hell?" David turned the light off and perked his ears to hear the sound again. Nothing was audible in the dark. Whatever had just moved past them was gone now. Then something in the distance caught his attention. "Hey, what's that?"

The others stood up and followed his gaze to the outlying field. Squinting, they noticed a faraway pair of white lights, moving slowly downward.

"Looks like a car," said Lance. "Probably driving down the mountain at the other end of the valley."

It did look like a pair of tiny headlights weaving its way down a mountain road. But then, surprising everybody, the two white lights separated. They each began their own dance in different directions.

"No way!" exclaimed Jaelyn, like a keyed-up child. "It's them! It's them!"

The crew stood still and stared at the faraway lights, involuntarily smiling in bewilderment. Several more lights appeared in the field, one at a time, some brighter than others. They varied in color—white, red, orange, and blue. Some drifted slowly; others were quick and energetic. The glowing orbs wandered all over the field, pairing up, separating, following, chasing.

"Amazing," said Jim. He had been skeptical about whether they would actually see these alleged ghost lights. But there they were, and he was taking them in with his own eyes. He searched his mind for a logical explanation for what he was seeing, but they were too bright at this distance to be fireflies. And nothing else could exude those different colors. He surrendered to the notion that the hypnotic lights really were ghosts.

Jaelyn was grinning from ear to ear. "Oh my God, this is so cool." She pulled Lance to her, kissed him, and then resumed watching the distant show.

"Come on," said Lance. "Let's get out there and see 'em up close."

CHAPTER 5
BURIAL GROUND

The group boarded the Honda, and Lance started the car. He pulled forward on the dirt road, navigating it into the broad field. After a hundred yards, the road curved ninety degrees to the left.

Lance followed the road left and kept his headlights on the dusty road. He was a little concerned that it was leading them away from where the spectral lights were. Hopefully, it would curve back to the right before long.

Jaelyn's eyes wandered to the darkness outside the passenger window. She noticed a long stretch of something white off to the right, about thirty feet from the road. It looked to be five or six feet tall and ran parallel to the road.

"Is that a fence?" she asked.

The others looked out and also saw the faint, white mass barely visible in the night. "Naw," said Jim. "Too solid. Looks more like a painted pipeline."

"Could be," said Lance. "I think there's a little bit of oil or natural gas that's extracted from the area."

"Huh," Karen grunted to herself. "I don't remember seeing that earlier today."

Lance switched on his high beams to better see the road before them. To his relief, he saw that it did turn to the right again. The Honda arrived at the second ninety-degree turn and followed it to the right. They were back on course, once again heading in the direction of the ghost lights.

In another hundred yards, the road abruptly ended. There was nothing in front of them but the dark field. Lance stopped the car and looked over at Jaelyn. "I guess this is where we get out." He turned off the headlights and engine, and the group stepped out.

They gathered in front of the car and looked out into the night. It only took a minute for them to spot a glowing orb. This one was soft blue and seemed to be the size of a cue ball. It was only thirty feet away from the crew.

"Ohmygod!" gushed Jaelyn. "Lookatit, lookatit!" Goosebumps were dancing on her skin.

A moment later, a second orb was seen. This one was white and slightly smaller than the blue one. It joined the other and began a slow orbit around it.

Karen was giddy. "They're so awesome up close!"

"Fuck yeah," muttered David. He felt like a little kid seeing something amazing for the first time.

The radiant spheres drifted, bounced, and dashed around the dark field, awing the spectators. Watching the ghost lights was everything the group had hoped it would be. It was magical. This was a night the students would remember for the rest of their lives.

A third orb appeared from somewhere in the field and floated toward the others. It was bright red and very intense. It circled its fellow orbs, corralling them. Then it moved them farther out into the field.

"Come on," said Jaelyn. "Let's go follow them."

Lance nodded. "I'm game." He looked at David. "Flashlight?"

"In the car, hang on," the Latino replied. He opened the rear door of the Honda and retrieved the flashlight from the floor. Then he handed it to his roommate. "Here ya go."

Lance turned it on and led his friends into the night. The bright beam lit the way, illuminating the field grass, sagebrush, and intermittent wildflowers. The group kept their eyes on the path before them as much as they could while looking up to watch the wandering lights.

Before long, the flashlight revealed a gravesite. A small, wooden cross was embedded in the dirt at a slight angle. The wood was dry and washed out, indicating its extreme age. Lance swung the light around and found several other grave markers nearby.

"Check it out," said David. "This must be the area where the 'bad souls' are buried."

"No," said Lance, remembering the sight from a distance when they had first seen the town. "I think those graves were closer to the church; we must've driven past them already."

"Well then," Jim chimed in. "These must be the really bad souls."

The notion made David uneasy. "Not funny, Jim." The Latino had a creepy feeling about these graves. They were all unmarked, with no names on the crosses.

The forgotten.

"Hey, the ghost lights are gone," said Karen.

The crew turned their attention to the night air around them. Sure enough, the bright orbs had vanished. Nothing but black.

A minute later, they detected a red glow in their peripheral vision. "There's one!" said Jaelyn. "The red one's back."

The red orb was drifting off to the side, heading away from the group. They followed, not wanting it to get too far from them.

Lance kept the flashlight aimed on the ground in front of them in order for the group to safely navigate the terrain. They walked for what felt like five minutes, weaving through the plants and rocks of the open field. Finally, the red orb stopped and hovered in place.

As the students tentatively stepped closer, the orb seemed to be waiting there for them. It was unafraid, almost inviting. The crew continued their advance. When they were a mere five feet from the spectral glow, it suddenly dissipated into nothing.

"Nooooo," Jaelyn pouted. "Where'd it go?"

"Bummer," said Jim. "We got *so close* to it! That was cool."

Sensing a particularly dark area just in front of them, Lance directed the flashlight from where they were standing to the dark spot below the red light's disappearance. The group was surprised to see a crater-like cavity in the ground, an eight-foot wide pit.

Like the "dead pit" the waitress mentioned, thought Lance. It definitely looked dead inside the rim, with no vegetation of any kind. Just sloped dirt and rock.

"Yikes," said Lance. "Glad we didn't accidentally fall into that." Then, after a few seconds of thought, he decided to explore the pit. "I'm gonna go check it out." He moved forward to the edge.

"Careful," Jaelyn said softly.

Lance grinned at her and cautiously stepped down the slope. It seemed pretty solid under his feet, and he had no trouble quickly getting to the bottom. He immediately noticed a sharp drop in temperature, and a puzzled expression graced his face.

Why is it so cold down here?

His flashlight showed the barren earth around him. Then he spotted an area where the dirt was dark and damp as if recently uncovered. It looked like small animals had been digging there. Lance looked closer and saw the corner of a plank jutting out. He gripped the corner and pulled, wriggling the plank loose from the dirt.

It appeared to be a grave marker. A name had been painted on it long ago, and enough of the paint was still barely hanging on to make the name legible.

BLACK JACK.

"Dude!" said Lance to the collective group above him. "It's a grave marker that says 'Black Jack'…you know, like the guy our waitress was talking about!"

Jim raised an eyebrow. "Cool, maybe that buried treasure is down there too."

"Come on down, guys," Lance invited. "If you want."

The others looked at each other, shrugged, and decided to join their friend in the crater. They had Lance illuminate the way while they climbed down single file. Then they gathered around him while he returned the light to where the plank was. He began to root around the area with his right foot.

Lance shifted his weight a little, and his left foot broke through the ground beneath. "Whoa!" he exclaimed, maintaining his balance. His foot dropped ten inches down into the earth.

"You okay?" Jaelyn asked.

"Yeah, just a little sinkhole or something." Lance pulled his foot out of the fresh hole and found more stable ground to stand on. Then he drew the flashlight's beam to the hole.

Something shiny reflected the light.

Karen noticed. "Hey, something's in there."

"I see," said Lance, nodding. Carefully, he knelt down for a closer look. There was something metal in the ground, exposed just enough to catch the light. Lance started pulling dirt away with his hands. In a few minutes, he could see what the object was.

"It's a latch on a wooden box," Lance announced. "Padlocked shut."

Jim got excited, his fantasy about finding treasure becoming more of a reality. "Lemme help!" He assisted in digging the dirt out of the area. Several large rocks were compacted into the ground, which made the removal that much harder. David put his hands to work as well, and eventually, the young men freed the object from its earthen prison.

It was an old box, no bigger than a car battery,

constructed of aged but sturdy wood. Being buried for so long had all but turned the wood black. The hinged lid was decorated with illegible carvings and held securely to the base with a steel plate, latch, and padlock.

"Holy crap, look at that!" said Karen, her eyes wide and bright. "Think there's anything inside?"

"Could be," Lance said. "It's heavy enough." He shook it but could hear nothing. "If there is, it's packed together so tight that nothing can move."

Jim felt a breeze picking up. He instinctively turned his face to it. "What do you all say we bring that thing back to the motel? We can open it there and have a few beers to celebrate our night."

The crew expressed their approval of the plan. They filed up the slope and out of the pit. Then they took a few minutes to search the field for a last glimpse of any glowing orbs. No more were visible in the plain. Satisfied with what they had already seen—and eager to see the contents of their discovery—they made their way back to the car.

Lance started the engine while everybody buckled in. Then he took a moment to turn the vehicle around and drove them back toward town. A hundred yards later, he saw the second ninety-degree turn they had encountered. He took it to the left and rumbled on, keeping his eyes on the dirt road.

"That big, white, pipeline thingy is gone," Karen said from the back seat.

Lance glanced to his left. "Huh. You're right. I don't see it anymore."

"It's got to be there," said Jim. "Stop the car, Bowser."

Lance had a better idea. "Hang on a minute." He

continued driving until they were back to the first ninety-degree turn. There he stopped and put the car in reverse. He cranked the wheel and maneuvered the CR-V until the high beams were aimed directly at where the white fixture should be.

Nothing was there. Instead of illuminating a vivid white object, the light from the headlights merely brightened the grassy foreground and dissolved into the darkness beyond.

"That's fucking weird," David mumbled.

"Indeed...," said Lance. He spent a moment trying to figure out why they could no longer see the stretch of white. Then his thoughts returned to the chest and its possible contents. "Whatever, let's get back to the motel. It's time for some beer and treasure!"

While his passengers cheered in agreement, Lance turned the car around and headed back toward the church. They drove past the cemetery, the old church, and the dormant baseball field, then finally reached the paved road.

Before long, they arrived at their motel. Lance parked the CR-V, and everybody spilled out. It was after one in the morning, so they tried to be as quiet as they could while traipsing upstairs to the suite. David unlocked the room, Lance carried the chest inside behind him, and the others brought up the rear.

Lance set the chest down on the dinette table while Jim went to the refrigerator for beer. The rest took seats at the table, fixated on the mysterious wooden chest. Jim arrived with an armful of cold beers and distributed them to his thirsty friends.

David pulled on the grimy padlock. "Damn. That lock is solid. We're gonna have to find something to bust it loose with."

Lance trotted to the kitchen to find something in the drawers that might be useful. But there was nothing in the room that could be used to open the lock. Disappointed, he returned to the table.

"Eh, we'll go borrow some tools from the motel owner tomorrow," Lance said with a shrug. "We'll get it open then."

Jim nodded. "'Til tomorrow then." He raised his beer to toast. "*Banzai!*"

"*Kanpai!*" Lance replied.

CHAPTER 6
THE CHEST

The group woke late the following morning. Despite their excitement about opening the wooden chest, the fatigue brought on by the long day and night before was too much. That and the amount of alcohol they'd consumed before finally turning in.

Lance opened his eyes, wincing at the daylight. He swung his legs over the edge of the bed and slowly sat up. "Ugh," he groaned. "I feel wrecked. What time is it?"

"Almost eleven," David replied. "We slept pretty late."

"Well sure," said Jim, "'cause we stayed up 'til three in the morning."

"Closer to four," Jaelyn said from the kitchenette. She and Karen had already dragged themselves out of their beds next door and come over for coffee with the men. "I can't believe we stayed up so late after such a long, busy day."

Yesterday had indeed been a lengthy day. Between the grueling twelve-hour drive from Tempe to Silver Valley, the late night chasing ghost lights, and the hours drinking and unwinding, it was a day that would have taken the wind out of anybody's sails.

Jaelyn emerged from the kitchenette with a steaming cup in her hand. "Coffee's ready," she announced, "and cups are right above it."

"Thank God," the rest said in near unison. They lined up, served themselves, and returned to the main living area. After letting the hot coffee slowly pull their senses awake, they studied the musty chest.

"Well," said David, "I don't see any screws. Looks like they used some kind of bolts or rivets. Even for the hinges."

"So we'll need something to cut the padlock," Lance added. "Or to pry the hardware off the wood."

"Or we just get an ax and chop the thing open," Jim offered.

"Sure," agreed Lance. "There's more than one way to skin a cat."

"I always hated that expression," said Karen.

"That's because your Indian name is 'Hugs Many Trees,'" Jim teased.

Karen could not help but giggle. "It is *not!*" Then she added, "It's 'Chokes Indian Jim.'"

Jim lifted his head. "You know I like a good choking."

"*Jim!*" Karen squeaked, her face turning red.

"All right, all right, you two," said Jaelyn, intervening. "I, for one, would love to see what's inside this chest."

"Me too," said David, standing up. "I'm gonna go see if the motel owner has any tools we can borrow."

Lance nodded. "Cool. See ya in a bit." Then he watched

his roommate exit the suite and pass across the window on his way down to the front desk.

David entered the front office and spotted the motel owner at the desk. "Hello," he smiled.

"How do?" the man replied, setting his cigarette on the astray behind him. "Didja go see your lights last night?"

"We did. It was really, really cool."

The owner grinned. "I reckon. Glad you kids had a fun time."

"So we were wondering," the Latino said, "if you have any tools we might borrow."

The man became concerned. "What for? You ain't plannin' any renovations on da room up there, are ya?"

David chuckled. "No, sir. Nothing like that. We just need something to bust an old padlock off a wood box."

"Hmm. I don't have any bolt cutters or anything like that, but you can try da claw hammer."

"Okay, that might work."

"Hang on a sec, I'll go get it for ya." The owner retreated into the room behind him and returned a minute later. "Here you go, son."

He handed over a hammer, and David took it. He noticed a name carved into the wooden handle and angled the tool in the light to read it. It was, MOREAU.

"I just wrote that so I can remember my name," the man joked. "Virgil Moreau. One of these days, I'm gonna hafta start writing my first name down too."

David chuckled at the man's dry humor. "Or just get a name plate for your desk."

"Hey, there ya go."

"Thanks, Mr. Moreau. We'll be sure to bring this back to you later."

"Alrighty then." The owner waved his hand and watched the youngster leave the office.

David returned to the suite with hammer in hand. His friends, still seated at the table, smiled optimistically upon seeing the tool. David offered it to Lance. "You wanna do the honors?" he suggested. "It's your find."

"Sure," Lance obliged. He took the claw hammer, turned it claw-side-down, and aimed for the wood tucked beneath the lock plate. The steel claw bit deeply into the old wood. Lance pried, wiggled, and yanked while a couple of the others held the chest down on the table. "It's getting loose," he announced, a glimmer of success in his voice.

Jim could only stare at the chest as Lance was working at the lock. He had no idea what would be inside. It could have contained gold, silver, deeds, maps, or anything else for that matter. He continued to grip the chest tightly.

The plate popped away from the lid. Everybody sat up straighter. The lid was loose, ready to lift open. The crew leaned forward, eager to see the reveal.

Teeming with excitement, Lance reached for the lid. "Here we go," he said. He pulled the wooden lid upward, and it creaked open like an animal waking from a long hibernation. The group was shocked when they saw the contents of the chest.

Instead of treasure, it was filled to the brim with scuttling, reddish-brown insects that appeared to be cockroaches.

Jaelyn squealed with fright, and the entire crew

instinctively jumped back. The bugs then sprang to life, spilling out over the chest like lava from an erupting volcano. They poured across the table and down the legs to the orange carpet.

Jaelyn jumped to the couch with the speed of a cheetah. The others continued stepping away from the table, and they watched in astonishment as the insects flooded the floor. There must have been a hundred of them.

"What the *fuck?*" Jim exclaimed. "What the holy *fuck?*" It was not possible that so many bugs could have come from inside that small chest. Not in a million years.

"Those are palmetto bugs," stated Karen, mesmerized.

"Those are goddamn *cockroaches!*" shrieked Jaelyn, her quivering feet rooted to the couch cushion.

"Yes," Karen explained, "but a different kind. I grew up with these on the East Coast. They're bigger than the cockroaches that live out here, and they need a warm, humid environment. Like Florida, Georgia, Louisiana, and such. Not like up here."

Jim was still staring at the swarming mass on the floor. "That's great and all, Professor Gives-A-Shit, but what the *fuck?*"

Then, as suddenly as they had escaped from the chest, the reddish-brown insects gathered in a tight group and scuttled up the table leg and back into the chest. By some miracle, the hundred insects were able to pack themselves neatly inside the wooden box. Then they lay together, disciplined and still except for the occasional shuddering of wings.

The stunned group gawked in awe. Their mouths

hung open, but they were speechless. Finally, Jaelyn broke the silence.

"*Shut it! Shut it!*"

Lance rushed to the chest and closed the lid. Picking it up and holding it shut tightly in his hands, he turned to David. "Gimme something to lock this up!"

The Latino shrugged. "What? Like duct tape?"

"Anything! Check the kitchen for something."

The crew rooted through the drawers and cabinets, looking for tape, twine, zip ties, anything. But their search yielded nothing that could be used to secure the wooden chest.

"Oh!" exclaimed David. "My belt." He hurriedly removed the belt from his jeans and brought it to his anxious roommate. "Here, move your hands over."

Lance tried to change his grip on the chest so his friend could wrap the belt around the middle. But his fingers slipped, and the box fell from his shaky hands. Everybody in the room gasped as the chest tumbled to the floor.

It landed on one of its top corners, and the lid broke completely off. Jaelyn shrieked, knowing what was to follow.

But nothing was inside. There was just an empty wooden box lying quietly on the carpet.

The group processed the sight for a moment, then tentatively leaned closer. "What the fuck...?" said Jim. "Where'd they go?"

"Wait a minute," David murmured, looking all around them. "That's not possible." He gazed at his stunned friends. "We all *did* see those bugs, right?"

The group nodded slowly. Then, baffled, they sat

down to reflect.

Feeling his gut suddenly clench from the excitement, Lance stood up. "I gotta go take a shit."

CHAPTER 7
ENCORE

The students collected themselves, contemplating whether they had all hallucinated or if they had actually witnessed something paranormal. Whatever the case, normalcy now seemed to be restored, and everybody was okay. They decided their best plan was to go on with their day as they had intended. At this point, they were starving, so lunch would be the first thing on their list. They showered and dressed in their separate rooms, regrouped in the suite, and then headed down to the car.

Jaelyn began a search for nearby restaurants on her phone. A few popped up, including a barbeque joint and the Italian place from last night, but none that sounded particularly appetizing for lunch.

"Let's just cruise Main Street and look around," suggested Jim. "I'm sure there's a deli or some little place where we could get brunch."

"Works for me," said Lance, starting the Honda and

letting the motor warm up for half a minute. Then he pulled out of the motel parking lot and drove the crew into town.

They caught sight of a bakery that had a dry-erase board advertising omelet brunch specials. The students thought that sounded like a winner, so Lance found a parking spot on Main Street and nestled in. The group stepped out of the car and walked into the eatery.

The scents of fresh pastries, muffins, and bacon combined to greet the crew when they entered. It was a pleasant mix, one that amplified their hunger. The group took an empty table and waited for a server to help them. A teenage girl came out to take their orders and was soon on her way back to the kitchen to relay the orders to the cook.

"So, what's our plan for today?" Jaelyn asked.

The students looked at each other with equal indifference. David offered the first suggestion. "I say we go back to the graveyard. And we can see if we can find that white pipeline thingy."

Lance bobbed his head earnestly. "Definitely. I want to see if that damn thing is really there or not."

"This is an old silver-mining town, right?" said Jim.

"Right," David affirmed.

"Then maybe after the graveyard, we could go driving around the area and check out the abandoned mines and stuff."

Karen was on board with that. "Totally. We could get some killer pictures of those."

"Cool," said Lance. "We have a game plan for the day. Then tonight, of course, we go back to the field and watch the ghost lights again."

"Of course," said David. "That's why we're here, after all. I'm excited to see an encore performance of what we saw last night."

A quiet minute passed before Jim asked the question that would not leave his mind. "So, are we not gonna talk about those bugs?"

Jaelyn squirmed. "Not before we eat."

"Wasn't that the craziest thing?" Karen gushed, ignoring her sorority sister's request. "That was super creepy."

"Fuckin' *ghost bugs*," muttered David. "We never expected to see something like *that*."

"We're definitely taking that chest back to school with us," said Karen.

"Indeed," Lance concurred, fascinated with the mysterious, aged chest. "The souvenir to end all souvenirs. Something my brother would totally get into."

Jaelyn remembered Lance telling her he had an older brother, but other than that, he was never brought up. "What's your brother do?" she asked.

"He does paranormal investigating. You know, like those TV shows with the ghost hunters. Except without the TV show."

"And not fake," David added.

Jaelyn was intrigued. "That's cool! Does he have a YouTube channel or a website?"

Lance shook his head. "I don't think so. He's pretty low-key. He has a Facebook page for his business, but that's about it."

"He still living somewhere in Texas?" queried David.

"Yeah, I'm pretty sure."

Jaelyn sensed an uncomfortable family vibe. "You're not very close to your brother, are you?"

David quietly watched his roommate while waiting for the response, but the expression on David's face indicated he already knew the story.

"Well," Lance began, "I'm not sure when it all started. He always felt like our parents treated him differently than they did me. Like he was the black sheep. Long story short, he never had a good relationship with our dad. And Dad *was* pretty tough on him. Finally, one day, they had one argument too many. Donnie figured enough was enough and left. My folks thought 'good riddance,' and haven't spoken to him since."

"Jesus," said Karen, shocked. "That's pretty hardcore."

"That's fucked up," Jim stated.

Jaelyn agreed. "That's terrible. I mean, I'm sure it's complicated, but I think family is too important to just throw away like that."

"Puts me in a difficult position," said Lance. "On one hand, I love my brother. But I love my parents. The best way to handle it is to just not talk about Donnie when I'm with my folks."

Jaelyn covered his hand with her own. "I'm sorry, sweetie, I had no idea."

"I know, it's okay." He smiled reassuringly. "Anyway, he'd *love* to hear about that old chest. This whole trip, for that matter."

"Maybe you can call him and tell him all about it when we get back."

"I should. It's been a while since we last chatted."

The food started coming out, the young girl delivering two plates at a time. The sight and smell of the brunch brought joy to the table. The hungry students ate heartily until they were full.

After their meal, and after restroom visits by those who needed them, the group boarded the Honda. Lance pulled onto Main Street and turned off a couple blocks later. He drove his friends past the neglected baseball field and back to the old church.

Lance parked on the shoulder of the dirt road. The crew exited the vehicle, their eyes drawn to the weathered church building. It sat old and tired, watching the visitors with plate-glass eyes. The students walked around the side of the church and made their way to the cemetery behind.

"Seems totally different here in the daytime," Lance remarked. In the bright daylight, the headstones and grave markers looked peaceful, almost comforting. Nothing sinister or spooky about them or the surrounding grounds.

"Yeah," said David. "But we'll see what it's like when we come back tonight after dark." He looked out across the field past the cemetery. "I don't see that white pipeline thingy."

Neither did the others. They saw the dirt road continuing in that direction, but then nothing but the valley basin terrain and the Amish houses at the far end. "We gotta get out there," Lance proposed, "and check it out up close."

The rest of the group was game, so they returned to the car and jumped inside. Lance took the dirt road farther out, just as he had done the night before. They quickly arrived at the first ninety-degree turn and followed it to the left.

"This was it," said Karen. "It was right out there, about thirty feet away from the road."

Nothing was there but sagebrush and yellow grass.

"A little strange," Lance admitted. He stopped the Honda and turned it off. "C'mon, let's get closer." The crew vacated the car and walked into the grassy field. They hoped to find evidence of some sort of structure out there, but they could not.

"Maybe it was fog?" asked Jaelyn, probing for an explanation.

Jim shook his head. "Naw, didn't have the conditions. It was neither cold nor humid here last night."

"One fact still remains," David stated. "That pipeline or solid fence — or whatever we thought it was — wasn't really there."

"So, what did we see, then?" asked Lance. "Like some kind of — *ghost fog?*"

David half-shrugged, half-nodded. "It's possible, I guess. I've never heard of that before, but if people have talked about ghost trains and ghost cars —"

"Or ghost horses," Karen added, thinking about the unseen horse and carriage they'd heard crossing the cemetery last night.

Jaelyn shuddered. "Ooh, now you guys are creeping me out."

"Yeah," said Jim, "like those stories we heard as kids about haunted objects that appear at midnight."

"Wasn't it around midnight when we drove out here and saw the white thing?" David asked.

"Could've been," Lance replied. "We were in the

cemetery for quite a while before that."

"So, what, then it disappeared after one?" said Jaelyn. "Like it was a 'witching hour' thing?"

Lance raised his eyebrows. "You never know."

Jaelyn looked out across the field once more. The only explanation for what they had seen last night was supernatural. A shiver flitted up her spine. "C'mon, guys, let's get out of here and find something fun to do."

"All right," smiled Lance, draping his arm over her shoulder. He escorted her to the car, opened the passenger door, and waited for her to climb in. The rest of the group followed suit, taking their seats inside the vehicle. Then Lance started the motor and turned them back toward the church.

Since they had plenty of time on their hands and were in a historic mining town, Jim repeated his suggestion to drive around and find the abandoned silver mines. They were not difficult to spot. The hills on the north side of town were littered with timber-reinforced openings and piles of excavated rock.

Lance drove toward the highest one he could see. The CR-V had no trouble navigating the rocky road leading to the mine site. Once Lance got them to the end of the trail, he parked the vehicle and smiled. "Let's go see a mine."

Stepping out, they saw old, blackened timbers lining the mouths of several entrances into the hillside. The students walked closer, stopping at the collar of one of the shafts. Rusty sections of rail ran into the shaft and disappeared into the pitch black. Knowing the mine was definitely not safe, the group had no plans to venture inside. But they were happy to take pictures of the foreboding sight, and they pulled out their phones to do so.

Then they wandered over to the enormous pile of crushed rock that had been removed from the mines during their years of operation. The crew filtered through the fragments, examining the different sorts of rock that had come from the earth. Karen took some close-up pictures of coarse pink granite and reddish-orange sandstone. Then she stood and faced her friends.

"Smile," she said, aiming at Lance and Jaelyn. The couple quickly posed, and Karen captured the image. "That's cute," she remarked.

David's eyes wandered across the landscape around them. The vast valley below seemed to breathe peacefully, its distant grasses dancing gently in the breeze. The lush mountain ranges surrounding the flatland provided a colorful contrast under the deep blue sky. "Man, it's beautiful up here," he said. The others followed his gaze and nodded.

Lance was truly awed by the majestic scene. "Indeed. This really is God's country."

"Well," said Jim, "we Indians still like to think it's *our* country."

Lance sneered. "You know what I mean."

"I do," Jim said with a grin. "But I also have to give you shit about your new friend in the heavens," he added, referring to Lance's recent adoption of the Christian faith.

Lance shrugged, guiltless. "It just makes sense to me. The New Testament does, at least."

"Hey, I'm not knocking you for your spiritual beliefs. If it works for you, then roll with it, *kemosabe*. The world might be a better place if more people had religion."

"Amen," added Jaelyn, who was not at all bothered by Lance's quest for spirituality.

And then Jim killed the poignant moment with his usual sarcasm. "Unless your religion involves terrorism and killing infidels."

"Of course," David said, playing along with the same candor in his voice. "That faction doesn't count."

"You're right about religion, though," Karen interjected. "I think the world could use more of it. Heck, just ask the Amish over there." She pointed to the small community barely visible at the end of the valley. "Religion has made their lives simple and peaceful."

"And boring," snorted Jim. "All right, c'mon, guys. What are we gonna go do next?"

The group made a loose plan for the rest of their day. They would drive around the region a little longer, check out some more old mines, go back into town, walk Main Street and peruse some of the shops, and then sit someplace for dinner.

After doing all those things, it was starting to get dark. The crew decided to buy more beer and return to the motel. There they would do a little bit of drinking to pass the time until it was dark enough to return to the cemetery.

It was around ten when they pulled up in front of the old church. Repeating the steps they had taken the night before, they made their way to the graveyard and eagerly scanned the black horizon for any ghost lights. Their eyes now trained for spotting them, it took no time at all for the group to see the first glowing orb.

"There's one!" said Jaelyn, as giddy as she was last

night. The others smiled and watched the floating orb. Soon others appeared to join in the nocturnal ballet. Jaelyn found Lance's hand and squeezed it tightly.

The students spent the next two hours enjoying the dancing of the mystical ghost lights.

CHAPTER 8
LEAVING TOWN

Lance heard a horse snorting in the distance.

He turned his head to see a barren hillside leading up from his position, perhaps fifty feet. At the top, against a fiery sunset backdrop, was a silhouette. It was the figure of a man wearing a cowboy hat, perched on a brawny horse.

Confused as to how he got there, Lance simply stood and stared at the mysterious figure. He waited for the man to say something, wave, or even move. But the man sat perfectly still atop his horse. Silent. Patient.

A wind began to pick up. It crept up from behind the rider and down the hill, gaining intensity and volume. Within seconds it grew from a whispering bluster to a roaring gust. It was unbearably loud by the time it reached Lance.

Lance's eyes snapped open.

It was morning, and he was lying in his motel bed.

He sat up and immediately felt woozy. Slowly the memories of last night returned to him. He recalled spending a couple of hours in the field watching the ghost lights dance around again, then the group returning to the motel, and finally playing drinking games until they were all out of beer.

Hearing Jim stir, Lance turned his head toward the couch. He immediately noticed the condition of the room. "What the hell…?" he slurred.

Jim focused his eyes to see what Lance was mumbling about. He was surprised to find the room in utter disarray. The wooden chest was still on the table, but everything else had been relocated. The dresser drawers were out, stacked sloppily on the carpet, and the men's clothes had been flung all over the room. Their suitcases were also open, the contents spread out across the floor. "Damn, dude," said Jim. "What happened here?"

"Did we get robbed?" Lance wondered. He got up from the bed and went to his pants on the chair. Feeling for his wallet, his fingers located it and pulled it from the back pocket. Lance opened it and found everything still inside. "Nope," he added, "doesn't look like it."

David woke and sat up in his bed. After rubbing his eyes, he noticed what his friends were going on about. "Damn, did we really drink *that* much?"

"I didn't think so," said Lance. "But with *us*, you never know."

"True story," Jim remarked. "I should never have taught you all drinking games."

Lance rolled his eyes and chuckled. Then he knelt down and began to pick up the scattered clothes. They needed to pack everything up this morning anyway, so now was a good enough time to start packing his suitcase.

After stowing everything except what he would wear today, Lance went to the kitchen and got a pot of coffee going. While waiting for it to brew, he leaned on the counter and watched his friends get their suitcases together. Jim winced and released a long, loud burst of gas. The smell permeated the room almost instantly.

"Dude!" exclaimed David, snarling at the horrible odor.

"What?" said Jim. "I gotta let it out. And it's not like the girls are in here."

Just then, there was a light knocking at the door.

"You were saying?" Lance smirked. Then he looked at David. "Turn on the ceiling fan, quick."

David flicked the switch on the wall, and the bladed fan above slowly began to turn. Then Lance went to the door and opened it, tentatively letting the young women inside.

Karen commented on the foul smell in the air. "Oh God, who farted? That's nasty."

David pointed to Jim. "Ask 'Farts Like Buffalo' over there."

Jim chuckled at both David's comment and his own embarrassing situation. He simply shrugged with a *whatcha-gonna-do* smile. Luckily the fan was effective, stirring the air enough to reduce the odor to a tolerable level.

The crew drank their allotment of coffee until they were fully awake. Then, keeping track of the time, the girls returned to their room to get showered and dressed before their eleven o'clock checkout. The guys took brief turns in their own shower and were soon ready for the day.

Their hands full with their possessions, the group

moved down the stairs to the ground level and across the parking lot to the car. Lance unlocked the vehicle and helped the others load everything inside. Then, while David, Jim, and Karen waited with the car, Lance and Jaelyn walked to the front office to check out.

The couple entered the office and found the owner seated behind his desk. They approached with the keys to the two rooms. The motel owner smiled cordially.

"Checkin' out, then?" he asked, standing to meet them.

"Yes," said Jaelyn, sliding the keys across the counter.

"Alrighty then," the owner acknowledged. "Enjoy your stay, did ya?" he added while picking up the room keys and looking up to face the guests. His smile locked tightly when he saw Lance, and Lance noticed. It almost seemed like the man recoiled a bit.

"We did, thank you," Jaelyn replied. "We had an awesome time watching the ghost lights. It was well worth the long drive to get here."

The man composed himself and continued the conversation. "Lotta folk come around to see that kinda stuff. I'm glad you got to see what you came for."

Lance felt a weird vibe from the motel owner. Why had he reacted so strangely when he saw Lance? The man continued to study Lance as subtly as he could while the students settled their bill.

"Thanks again," said Lance when the checkout was complete. He eyed the owner one more time and smiled.

The man smiled back. "My pleasure. Y'all drive careful, now." He kept his curious gaze on Lance while the couple left the office.

Lance stopped as soon as they were outside, touching Jaelyn's arm to catch her attention. She turned to him in response.

"Do I look okay?" he asked.

Jaelyn visually scanned him. "Yeah, why?"

"The guy there kept looking at me funny. Like I had something on my face."

"Naw, you're good. Just plain ol' Lance." She smiled and winked, walking past him into the parking lot.

Shrugging, he followed her and met up with the others. The group boarded the Honda, and Lance started the motor. He steered out of the parking lot and onto Main Street. After a quick stop to fill the gas tank, Lance headed east out of town.

He glanced out at the field as they left Silver Valley. He saw what appeared to be a rider on a horse in the distance. The figure was sitting motionless atop his perch. Though he was too far away for Lance to see his face, Lance could tell that the rider was watching him. A quick look to the road to make sure he was still in his lane, and then Lance returned his eyes to the field.

The rider and horse were gone.

Weird, thought Lance. *Am I going nuts?*

After convincing himself that he had mistaken some rocks and brush as a figure on a horse, he focused his mind on completing the twelve-hour trip back to Arizona.

CHAPTER 9
HOUSEKEEPING

The motel owner ate the last of his peanut butter sandwich and washed it down with room-temperature milk. All of his guests that were leaving today had checked out, so he was alone in the quiet office. He looked up at the clock to see it was after one. Now that he had finished his lunch, it was time to start cleaning the rooms.

Making sure the answering machine was on, he vacated the desk and brought his dishes to his room in the back. Then he grabbed an armful of clean linens from the dryer and brought them out to the office. He picked up his keys, left the office, and locked the door behind him.

What was wrong with that kid? he kept thinking. Something about the young man who checked out didn't seem right. He *looked* normal, but the motel owner could detect — could *feel* — something wrong with the boy's face. Like two different people were looking back at him through the same eyes. Impossible, he knew, but the feeling had been lingering with him ever since.

Stopping by the supply room, he unlocked it and retrieved his vacuum and bucket of cleaning supplies. Then he continued his trek to the stairs. He would start on the second floor, in the suite where the students had stayed.

When he opened the door, he was greeted by a chill. He figured it was from the air conditioner, cranked up and left running by the guests. No big deal, he would turn it off and save some electricity. He went to adjust the air conditioning unit but saw that it was already off. The motel owner frowned; he definitely felt cold air in the room. Had the kids left a window open? He checked the windows to find them all closed and locked.

Without giving it any more thought, he focused on the job at hand. He set the linens on the couch and brought the cleaning supplies to the kitchenette. Spotting a hammer on the linoleum counter, he looked closer. He recognized the familiar tool with his surname carved into the handle.

"There ya are, Mr. Moreau." He chuckled, wondering what on earth those crazy kids had used the hammer for. Needing to move it from there so he could clean, he took the hammer from the counter and placed it on the table.

Returning to the kitchenette, he began spraying the counters with Windex. He wiped them down, rinsed the coffee pot and cups, and loaded the dishwasher. Then he gave the floor a quick once-over with a cleaning rag. The kitchen done, he turned his attention to changing the bedsheets. He walked past the table on toward the beds.

He heard a light raking sound behind him.

Turning around, he saw nothing in the room but the

couch and table. And his hammer was gone.

"What da hell?" he mumbled, bending down to see if it had slid off the table and landed on the carpet. It was not there either.

Scratching his head, he looked at the kitchenette counter where he knew he had seen it before. No hammer there.

Whatever, he thought. There were rooms to be cleaned, and he wanted to waste no time getting them done.

Humming a little tune, he stripped the beds and tossed the covers aside in a heap. Then he took the first sheet from his pile of linens and began stretching the fresh cotton onto the mattress.

The hammer appeared from behind the couch, slowly floating upward. It stopped and remained suspended in midair for a second before suddenly flying across the room and striking the back of the owner's skull.

A bright flash of white shot through the man's vision upon impact. With a yelp, he toppled forward onto the mattress. The hammer rose above its victim, turned its clawed side down, and came down hard. The steel embedded itself deeply, penetrating bone and the brain tissue beneath.

The chill in the room then drifted out the open door and dissipated into the quiet sky.

PART II

CHAPTER 10
DISTURBING NEWS

Lance dreamed about the man on horseback. At the top of a fifty-foot hill, the dark silhouette sat motionless while focusing on Lance, who was standing below him in a field. Silent and still, the man in the cowboy hat simply studied Lance.

The sun had settled behind the mountains, leaving nothing but a veil of pink and orange in the sky behind the shadowy figure. Lance focused on the mysterious rider. He could see nothing but a dark shape, but still, the man seemed familiar. Lance had the strangest feeling that this man knew him.

A bellowing wind could be heard in the distance. It quickly drew nearer, coming from the horizon behind the rider. The gust blew over the hill, past the man and horse, and came rushing down toward Lance. It grew louder, stronger, as it closed on him. The deafening wind was almost upon him when he woke.

He saw the familiar surroundings of his bedroom and realized he was back in his apartment in Tempe, Arizona. He could hear his phone ringing on the other side of the door, and he remembered leaving it in the living room to charge. Grumbling, he rose from the bed and opened the door. He hurried to the phone on the coffee table and answered it.

"Hello?"

"Is this Lance Bowser?" said a man with a robust voice.

"Yes, who's this?"

"This is Sheriff Bill Skelton calling from Venture County."

Lance did not know where that was. "Okay...."

"Were you and some friends recently in Silver Valley, staying at the Valley Inn?"

"Ah yes," confirmed Lance. "We left there yesterday and got home late last night."

"Could you confirm when you left yesterday?" the man asked.

An uncomfortable feeling swept through Lance. "What's this all about?"

"Well," the sheriff announced, "Virgil Moreau, the owner of the motel, was found dead late last night."

"Oh my God!" Lance exclaimed, stunned. "Are you sure?"

"Um, yeah, we're pretty sure."

"I mean, it's just that he seemed perfectly healthy yesterday when we checked out. I'm shocked to hear that he's dead."

"More than just dead, I'm afraid," said the sheriff. "He's been murdered. Wounds indicate the weapon was something like a claw hammer."

"Shit."

"And as you can imagine, we need to ask everybody that was staying there for information."

"Of course," Lance said, unknowingly nodding. He sat down on the couch.

"So," the lawman continued, "could you confirm when you left yesterday?"

Lance closed his eyes. "Um, we checked out right around eleven. Then we gassed up the car and hit the road."

"Ah. And your friends' names?"

"We're not *suspects* or anything, are we? I mean, come on, we *loved* that funny old guy!"

The sheriff softened his voice. "No, son. Not at this point. I just need to know who all was there, question them, and gather information. Strictly routine in an investigation like this. Besides, if what you say is true, you left a couple hours before the estimated time of death."

"Okay."

"So, who all was with you?"

Lance provided the names of his friends, confirming the spelling of some. The sheriff asked if Lance saw or heard anything that could aid him in solving the crime. Lance had nothing for the lawman to use. Then Lance enquired about who found the body, when, and where, and Sheriff Skelton provided all the answers he had.

When the sheriff was ready to end the call, he said, "I'll let you go now — sorry to bring you the disturbing news. Call me if you can think of anything helpful to the investigation, anything at all."

"Okay, will do," said Lance, his vacant stare fixed on an empty beer can left on the coffee table.

"And make sure you and your friends stay available in case I need to reach any of you."

"Of course. I always have this phone."

"All right. Have a good day, Mr. Bowser."

"Goodbye." Lance hung up and gawked at the phone for a minute, still processing the conversation he just had. Then the door to David's bedroom opened, and Lance's roommate emerged.

"Who was that?" David asked, rubbing his eyes.

"Dude…you know that guy who ran the motel we just stayed at?"

"Yeah."

"Well, he's dead. That was the sheriff up there in Colorado."

David was suddenly wide awake. "What? No way!"

"Yeah, killed by someone with a hammer."

"Jesus," muttered David. "That's horrible. He was a cool guy."

"Want to know the creepiest part?" Lance said, eyebrows raised.

"What's that?"

"His body was found in the room we were staying in."

A chill trickled down David's spine. "Oh man, that's messed up. The same room we were sleeping in…."

"I know, right? Crazy."

"Who found the body?"

"One of the guests happened to look inside the open room passing by it last night. The light was on, and they saw the body lying on the floor," said Lance, repeating what the sheriff had told him. "I'm guessing they called the police right after that."

David ambled to the kitchen to start the coffee maker. "The cops don't think we had anything to do with it, do they?"

"I don't think so. He just said he had to question all the guests that were there. Plus, he said the time of death was a couple hours after we checked out."

"Yeah, I don't think we'll be going back to *that* town again."

Lance gazed blankly at the floor. "No, I don't think so." He lifted his eyes to his roommate. "We'll have to tell the others."

"Speaking of the others," said David, "what are our plans today?"

"I dunno, why?"

"I was just thinking we should all go do something together." He flashed a blatantly broad smile. "And Karen definitely has to come along."

Lance chuckled. "I see."

"We should see if they wanna go swimming. Or sunbathing. Or anything that involves bikinis."

"You're subtle."

David shrugged. "You can't deny they both have great bodies. Attraction is unavoidable."

"I can't argue with you there," admitted Lance. "But that's not the only reason I asked Jaelyn out. She's got a sweet personality, and her smile just makes me happy."

"Bleh. So, are you hittin' that yet or not?"

"Dude!" Lance blushed a little. He had not yet taken

his girlfriend to bed, although he very much wanted to. "I don't want to rush her, you know that."

"I get that, but come on. She's a sorority girl—and a hot one—so I'm sure she's not afraid of sex."

Lance defended his chivalrous position. "Look, she's beautiful, smart, makes me laugh…she's special. I don't want to do anything before she's ready. I don't want to scare her away."

David lifted his hands from the counter and held them up. "All right, all right. Whatever makes you happy." He glanced back at the coffee maker. "Coffee's ready."

"Thank God," said Lance. He got up from the couch and walked to the kitchen counter. "You know, I don't think I could live without coffee."

David handed him a cup, poured his own, and then gave the pot to Lance. The friends drank their hot coffee and thought about what they wanted to do that day.

CHAPTER 11
BLACK JACK GRAINGER

The man was there again.

Lance was back in the field, at the bottom of the hill, looking up at the silhouette on the horse. The sun was setting fast, leaving nothing but a faint veil of orange in the sky behind the rider. Lance had been in this dream several times before, and he realized that. Not as apprehensive as he was before, he called out to the stranger to identify himself.

The rider shifted in his saddle. Then, tilting his head ever so slightly, his eye was visible, not in detail, but rather a single glowing eye in the dark silhouette of the man's head.

Lance was mesmerized by the light of the eye. All he could do was stand motionless while locking eyes with the man. He heard the familiar sound of the wind building, growing, and gusting down the hill toward him, but he was powerless to react. By the time the roaring wind hit Lance, he expected to wake from what he now knew was a dream. But instead of snapping awake at the moment of impact, Lance suddenly saw nothing but gray.

No images, no sounds; nothing but — *gray.*

After an uncomfortably long time, Lance finally came to. It took him a moment to comprehend that he was in his bedroom, not in that unsettling gray hell. He drew several long breaths to soothe himself, then sat up.

He felt drained — like a hangover but without a headache. That could not be the case, though, as he had not drank an excessive amount of alcohol the night before. Just a few beers while playing video games with his roommate. Nevertheless, he was weary. Shaking the cobwebs from his head, Lance got up and walked to the kitchen.

David was seated in the living room, watching TV and drinking coffee. Lance acknowledged him and poured himself a cup of hot brew. Then he joined his roommate on the couch.

"Yo," said David.

"Mornin'," Lance replied, straining his eyes to focus on the clock. "At least I hope it still is."

"It is. What are you gonna do today?"

Lance shrugged. "I dunno. Jaelyn wants to go get textbooks today, so I told her I'd meet her at the bookstore this afternoon."

"Sounds like a blast."

"You?"

"Eh. I feel like just chillin' out here today and doing nothing. Won't get too many more chances before classes start."

"No lie," said Lance, sipping his coffee. He frowned, the image of the rider in his dream still fresh in his mind.

"You know, I've had the weirdest dreams lately."

"Yeah?" David grinned. "About kinky stuff with Jaelyn?"

"No dude, I'm serious. There's this man on horseback, on top of a hill. I can't see his face, but I've had the same dream a few times. Started back when we were in that motel in Silver Valley."

"Maybe it's that Black Jack guy," said David. "Pissed off that you took his old wooden box."

Lance raised an eyebrow. "You know, that would be creepy as shit. But I *couldn't* be dreaming about him since I've never even seen him."

"We should get online and check him out," David suggested. "Now, I'm a little curious to see if there are any pictures of him."

"Good idea," replied Lance. He went to his bedroom, retrieved his laptop, and brought it back out to the living room.

When the computer was powered up and connected to the Internet, Lance began his search. Not knowing the man's full name, he just typed "Black Jack cowboy Silver Valley" in the search box and scrolled through the results that popped up.

"Ah, here he is," Lance announced. The link he spotted was about Black Jack Grainger, a killer in Silver Valley, Colorado.

David craned his neck to see the screen. "Any pictures?"

"Let's see," said Lance. He typed in "Jack Grainger" and set the search filter for images. Dozens of old black-and-white pictures populated the screen. Most were of a stern-faced man with a dark mustache. He appeared to be in his thirties when the photographs were taken.

"That's him, huh?" David commented. "Looks a little creepy."

He did indeed. Lance could see something in the man's face — something in his eyes — that was dark. Evil. And despite not being able to see the face of the man in his dream, Lance had a strong feeling this was the same man.

"Ooh, click on that one," said David, pointing to a grainy image of a mass grave.

Lance opened the picture and subsequent link to the associated webpage. The page featured an article titled "THE LEGEND OF JACK GRAINGER." Lance began to read it out loud.

"'Few historical figures from the Old West have left a black mark like Jack Grainger. An orphan raised by a rancher, he left at a young age to join the army in 1870. His service was brief, however, as his violent conduct quickly led to his dismissal with an Other Than Honorable Discharge. He was said to have scalped dozens of Indians, including women and children.'"

"Damn, took his job seriously."

"Right? Check this out. 'In the years that followed, Grainger roamed the West, leaving his brutal mark on each town he visited. No longer applying his murderous skills only to Indians, he began killing whites, blacks, and Chinese as well.'"

David nodded. "Equal opportunity," he tittered.

Lance continued to read. "'Grainger is rumored to have murdered dozens of people over the next ten years. Some he scalped, others he skinned. His grotesque killings soon earned him the nicknames 'Jack the Skinner' and 'Black Jack.'

"'The law closed in on him in 1880, ambushing him inside a saloon. A huge struggle ensued. Grainger was able to kill the four deputies and escape, but not without injury. He lost his left eye to the knife of one of the deputies, giving him the new nickname 'One-Eyed Jack.'" Lance stopped and said, "Shit."

Now there was no question in his mind. This man, Jack Grainger, *had* to be the character haunting his dreams. The single eye detail could not be a coincidence.

"This is the guy in my freakin' dreams!" Lance stated fervently. The look on his face was one of confusion and fear.

David did not know how to respond. "That's crazy, dude."

Lance sat numb for a moment. He *must* have seen this man's face before, perhaps one of the forgotten memories from a history class long ago. There could be no other explanation. Lance accepted that and then returned his attention to the article.

"'Fate finally caught up with him in 1882. After skinning a prospector from Louisiana, he was killed by the man's sister. The woman, Estelle Toutant, got word of her brother's vicious murder and traveled to Colorado to find his killer. Nobody knows how she found and captured Grainger, but witnesses saw her put him to death and burn his body. His burnt remains were placed inside a wooden chest and buried somewhere in the outskirts of Silver Valley, the budding mining town he died in.'"

"Wooden chest?" David echoed. "Like the one we dug

up and opened?"

Lance nodded, having the same disturbing thought. "Very possible," he said, looking toward his bedroom. He could only imagine the sordid history of the unearthed chest on his dresser. He shuddered.

Taking another sip of his coffee, Lance went back to his image search. He took in the images of the notorious Black Jack Grainger, his eyes pausing on each picture to study the face of this mysterious man.

The man looked calm in each photograph but solemn. There was purpose in his eyes. He wore just the hint of a scowl beneath his black handlebar mustache. To think that this man was capable of the horrific acts he committed was unsettling to Lance.

And, in a small way, fascinating.

CHAPTER 12
THE FRAT BOY

Jaelyn slung her purse on her shoulder, donned her sunglasses, and went outside. Tilting her head up to acknowledge the bright sun, she made her way down the porch steps and to the sidewalk. She continued west toward the college campus.

The ASU campus was fairly busy with students roaming to and fro. With classes beginning in a couple of weeks, this was when many of the students were out to purchase the books and supplies they would need for the fall semester.

Jaelyn passed Armstrong Hall, Ross-Blakley Hall, and the Phys. Ed. East building on her way to the campus bookstore. She reached her destination and looked around for Lance. He was not there yet. She looked at her watch, realizing she was there a little early. Lance would be along shortly, so she would just wait for him outside.

While she waited and watched the other students wander past, Jaelyn felt a cold breeze. But unlike an ordinary breeze, this one seemed to sweep around her twice before blowing past. She sensed something...odd about it.

"Hey, Jaelyn!"

Jaelyn turned her head to see who was addressing her, and her stomach clenched when she saw him. *Oh God, there's Todd.*

It was Todd Ryan, a young man she wished had never been a part of her life. Todd was a fraternity brother in the Beta Theta Pi house, which was where she met him. They'd gotten together a year ago during a frat party and did the things that young drunks do at frat parties.

Regret was there the following morning, and she crept out of his bedroom before he could wake. She made it back to her sorority house and took a long, hot shower. It was not like her to sleep with a man she had just met. She was ashamed of herself, although she admitted she had enjoyed the night.

The following weeks were awkward whenever she ran across Todd on campus. He wanted to see her again and made mention of that each time he encountered her. But Jaelyn politely — and repeatedly — informed him that she was not wanting to date anybody. She told him their drunken night together was a mistake.

That night left her pregnant. She did not know she was carrying until almost two months later when she had a miscarriage. The realization that she had just lost a life that was growing inside her shook her. The most devastating part was that she never even knew she was pregnant. There had been no morning sickness, no tenderness in her breasts, and no increased urination. She was late on her menstrual cycle, but that was something her body had done to her before.

The last thing she wanted to do was tell Todd. It would only make him think about her more than he already did. Plus, there was nothing he or anyone else could do about it. She decided the best thing for her to do was not tell anybody about the baby she had lost. Best to just move on as if it never happened.

Now that he had spotted her again, he smiled. The spry, blond-haired young man trotted across a greenbelt to join her. "Hey, Jaelyn, how've you been?" he said when he got to her.

"Hi, Todd," she replied cordially. "I've been pretty good. You?"

"Great! Just got back from Maui with my folks. It was awesome."

"Cool."

"How 'bout you? Whatcha been up to this summer?"

"Not much." Jaelyn only offered short, uninviting responses. Hopefully, Todd would get the hint and go about his business. She was not that lucky.

"Hey, we're having a killer party at the house this weekend. You should come. It'll be awesome."

"Eh, I'm kinda partied out."

Todd was not giving up that easily. "Well, how about we go out and do something tonight? Whatever you like."

"Sorry, Todd," Jaelyn stated. "I'm seeing somebody. So there's that."

***

Lance was watching from a distance. Having just passed the student recreation complex and rounding the intramural field, he paused behind a tree when he spotted

Todd with Jaelyn. *What's he doing talking to her?* he wondered. He knew Todd had a thing for his girlfriend, and he knew she had always kept the frat boy at bay.

Despite wanting to insert himself between the two, Lance elected to wait unseen until Todd was gone. He was intimidated by Todd. The frat boy was handsome, with wavy blond hair and tan. But he was also a muscular athlete. He was bigger than Lance, and Lance knew he was Todd's physical inferior. Lance would hang back until the frat boy left.

After a moment, Todd gave Jaelyn a friendly little wave and walked away. Once he had disappeared from sight, Lance resumed his journey toward the bookstore. He took his time making his way to Jaelyn, giving her a smile when she finally caught sight of him approaching.

"Hey, you," he said. "I hope you haven't been waiting long."

Jaelyn embraced him when he arrived. "Nope, not long." She gave him a kiss. "Well, should we get this mess over with?"

"I reckon," he replied. He took her hand, and they walked into the bookstore to hunt down the textbooks they would need for the upcoming semester's classes.

It took half an hour to round up the books they required. They were lucky enough to find some that were used, which they preferred for two reasons: they were cheaper, and the important passages had already been highlighted or underlined. The rest of the necessary textbooks were only available as new — and more expensive — copies.

They stood in line, paid for their requisite books, and exited the bookstore. Once outside, they were relieved to have that task behind them. They were hungry now. The couple visited Memorial Union to get something to eat.

After sitting at a table with their meals, they commenced wolfing down their early dinners. Lance swallowed his first bite, then looked Jaelyn in the eye. "So, what do you want to do tonight?" he asked.

Jaelyn shook her head gently while sipping iced tea through her straw. "I'm sorry, sweetie, I have to do this thing with my sorority sisters tonight."

Lance was deflated. "Oh. What are you doing?"

"Just the usual silly rush stuff with the new pledges."

"Okay." Lance tried to sound understanding, but he could not hide the disappointment in his voice.

"I'm sorry," she repeated, following up with a reassuring smile. "How about I come over to your place tomorrow night to make it up to you?"

He nodded. "Sure. That sounds cool."

"Hey, did you see the pics I posted?"

Lance had not checked his social media since yesterday. "No, not yet."

"Here," said Jaelyn, pulling the website up on her phone. She tapped the app, and her homepage popped up. Then she opened the album she had marked "SILVER VALLEY WEEKEND" and slid the phone over to Lance. "Check 'em out. They turned out nice."

Lance browsed through the photo album, and the images made him grin. He saw a few shots of the graveyard when they first drove in, then a couple of the small town's rustic Main Street buildings, followed by pictures of the group drinking and laughing in the motel room. When he saw a photo of the late motel owner, he frowned.

"You may want to delete this one," Lance stated.

Leaning over, Jaelyn's face grew white. "Oh shit. I forgot he was in there." She had posted these pictures yesterday morning before Lance had informed her of the motel's owner's gruesome murder.

"If the police are going through our profiles, seeing a pic of him might make them more prone to suspecting us."

"Done," she said, deleting the photo.

Lance perused the rest of the online album to see what other photos she had taken. He came across a shot of the field. He remembered the area well, spotting where they had seen the floating lights and where the pit was found. A chill wiggled up his spine.

***

Eventually, it was time for Jaelyn to get back to the sorority house. She said goodbye to Lance with a long, sweet kiss. Then she began the walk home.

When she arrived at the house, she dropped her textbooks off in her room. Figuring her phone's battery was low, she set the phone on its charger. Then she devoted her attention to getting ready for the activities ahead.

The house sisters assembled in the living room, along with three new pledges. The evening began with each pledge quickly having to learn the names of each sister and something about them. Then the pledges had to wear silly costumes and go out with their big sisters, knocking on the doors of the surrounding Greek houses to introduce themselves and sing a song.

It was almost midnight when Jaelyn was ready for

bed. After a night of fun goofiness and a few glasses of wine with her sorority sisters, it was time to turn in. Jaelyn said goodnight to her housemates and vanished upstairs to her bedroom.

She wanted to hear some music. After brushing her teeth and slipping into her sleepwear, she brought her headphones from the desk to the bed. She plugged into her phone, opened her playlist, and let the music flow into her ears.

Mellow alternative music was playing. It helped her release her thoughts and drift off to unconsciousness. Just before she was about to fall asleep, her ears registered a voice she had not heard before. It was a speaking voice, deep and faint, saying something just beneath the sound of the song's music and lyrics.

"Unborn child," she thought it said.

Her eyes popped open. *What the hell?* she mused. *That's not part of the song.* Furrowing her brow in the dark, Jaelyn tapped the button to jump to the next track.

A different song started playing, and Jaelyn closed her eyes again. The words were still on her mind. They made her think of the miscarriage that resulted from her night with Todd. She fought to concentrate on the music instead.

The ghostly voice returned. "Unborn child," it said again, just audible over the music in her headphones.

She tensed and sat up in her bed. The voice was real; she had now heard its eerie message twice. She felt terror. Looking around the room in the light from her phone's screen, she saw nothing unusual about her surroundings. Jaelyn looked at the playlist on her phone, and it innocently displayed the collection she had put there long ago. She pulled the headphones off and tossed her phone across the room onto the pile of dirty clothes.

She no longer wanted to hear any music. She wanted to hear nothing at all.

CHAPTER 13
SEEING THINGS

Lance did not want to open his eyes the following morning. He had just woken but could not find the will to pry his eyelids apart. It took ten minutes for him to finally stir.

He sat up slowly and swung his legs over the side of the bed. Then he held that position for a moment, palms on the edge of the mattress, and took note of how tired he was. He was exhausted. Looking at the clock on the nightstand, he realized he had slept for a sufficient amount of time. He should not feel this weak—maybe he was getting sick.

With great effort, he rose from the bed and stood. The motion caused something to fall off the mattress and land on the floor with a *clack*. Lance bent down enough to see what the small object was.

It couldn't be.

He rubbed his eyes. There was no way he saw what he thought he had. He looked again, straining to focus better.

Sure enough, he was gazing at what appeared to be an

eyeball resting on the floor.

His body tensed. "What the hell...?" he muttered. He lowered himself to the floor and tentatively reached out to pick it up.

It felt like a light rock in his hand. Drawing it closer to his face, he was able to study the mysterious object in detail. It definitely looked like a human eyeball. But it was petrified, hard and glazed. Lance shuddered. But then his terror gave way to curiosity. Where the hell did it come from? He had never *seen* anything like this, much less brought it into his room.

For a second, it made him think of Jack Grainger's missing eye.

Lance suddenly felt woozy. He set the item safely on his desk to investigate later. Right now, what he needed was a glass of water to quench his parched body. And then some coffee to stimulate his system. He opened the bedroom door and headed toward the kitchen.

David was up, sitting in front of the television. "Morning, sleepyhead," he said when he saw his roommate. "Coffee's made."

"Awesome," Lance croaked. He walked to the sink and poured himself a glass of water. After gulping it down, he pulled his coffee mug from the counter and filled it with steaming coffee. Then he joined his friend on the couch to watch whatever made-for-TV movie was on.

"You okay?" asked David, noting the dull expression on Lance's face.

"Yeah, I'm just wiped out. I feel like I could sleep for an entire day."

David shrugged. "Go for it if you need to. I hope you're not sick."

"No, man, I don't feel sick. Just…tired."

"You didn't drink that much with me last night," noted David, "so you shouldn't be hung over." He raised his eyebrows. "Maybe you just stayed up too late thinking about Jaelyn?"

"Nope," Lance declared. "I fell asleep pretty much right after I went to bed." He held up his index finger. "She is coming over tonight, by the way, now that you mentioned her."

"Here?" said David, and Lance nodded with a subtle grin. "Cool. Maybe you'll finally get to sleep with her."

Lance was too weary to consider the idea of sex, but he did not reject it. "We'll see," was all he said.

"Well," said David, "it turns out you'll have the place to yourselves for a while. So, this might be a good night for the two of you."

"Yeah? Where are you gonna be?"

The Latino sat up straight and proud. "I've got myself a date with Karen."

"No way!" Lance was happy for his friend, knowing how strongly David felt about Karen. "That's awesome, man."

David flaunted an exaggerated smile. "Yep, she finally succumbed to my charms."

"That's cool," said Lance. "I'd like to see the two of you get together. Karen's really cool."

"I'd like to see us 'get together' too," David winked.

"Dude!" exclaimed Lance, the wink reminding him of the morning's find. "You have to see what I found in my bedroom this morning!"

"It better not be a dead hooker."

It was too early for humor, but Lance chuckled anyway. "No, I'm totally serious."

"What is it?"

Lance curled his toes. "I think it's an eyeball."

David shrank back. "Whaaaat?"

"Come on, you gotta take a look."

Urging his roommate to get up, Lance brought David to his bedroom. He turned the light on and approached the desk. The spot where he had placed the eye was vacant. He moved papers aside to locate the missing item. It was nowhere on the desk. Lance looked on the floor next, but the eye was not there either. Frowning, he faced his unconvinced roommate.

"Ha ha," said David. "You got me."

"No!" Lance protested, his open hand aimed at the desktop. "It was right here! I set it right *here*, not more than ten minutes ago."

"Whatever, dude. If you find it again, you can show it to me."

Befuddled, Lance surrendered and returned to the living room with David. They settled into the couch, drinking coffee and watching TV. Despite trying to focus on the movie, all Lance could think about was the old, hardened eye. He couldn't have imagined it; he vividly remembered the look, the weight, the *feel* of it...it had to be real. So, where did it go?

Maybe One-Eyed Jack took it back, he thought sarcastically.

The afternoon was spent lazing in front of the television and snacking on whatever munchies the pair had. Eventually, it was time for the roommates to get ready for their respective evenings. Lance took a shower and dressed. While he was heading out to the grocery store, David showered and primped for his date with Karen.

Lance had the pasta boiling and the garlic bread in the oven by the time Jaelyn arrived. She set a bottle of wine on the table and walked into the kitchen to kiss him. The aroma of the spaghetti sauce brought a look of delight to her face. "My God, that smells good," she said.

"Just the way my grandma showed me. It's all about how you cook the hamburger. Some Worcestershire, a little beer, and then fennel seed for that Italian sausage flavor."

She looked astounded. "I would never have thought to cook meat with beer, but I trust you."

He plated and served their dinner while Jaelyn opened the bottle and poured the red wine. They sat together and enjoyed the meal Lance had prepared. He was astonished by how hungry he was; he ate two platefuls.

After placing the dishes in the sink, the couple migrated to the living room. Jaelyn produced the DVD she had brought for their evening's viewing, and she put it on. They refilled their wine glasses, nestled together on the couch, and watched the romantic comedy.

When the movie was over, she gazed at Lance and noticed something was off with him. "You okay?" she enquired.

He turned to her. "Yeah, of course." He added a smile. "Why do you ask?"

"Nothing, you just seem like you're preoccupied."

"I'm sorry, I don't mean to." Lance held her hand. "I'm totally fine, just had some weird things happening lately."

"Like what?"

Lance was unsure of telling her what was on his mind, but then he realized she would not mock him for it. She was a good, caring person. He could open himself to her.

"Well," he began, "I've been having strange dreams the last few nights. About a strange cowboy on a hill. I can't see his face, but I know he's looking at me. And it's like he knows me."

"That's creepy," said Jaelyn.

"And then this morning, I found what looked like an eyeball."

Jaelyn tensed. "What? Where?"

"On the bedroom floor. It looked old, like a fossil."

"Can I see it?" she whispered.

Lance sighed. "Nope. When I tried to show David, it was gone. Just disappeared. Like it was never there."

Jaelyn thought for a minute. "I wonder if you're just stressed out. I mean, after our trip to the mountains, seeing ghosts, then hearing about the motel owner being killed. Plus, we have classes starting back up soon."

He was receptive to her theory. "Could be."

"I know what will take your mind off it," she said, twirling her hair with her finger.

"Yeah? What's that?"

Jaelyn moved closer, taking his face in her hands. She kissed him deeply. As their kissing grew more passionate, Jaelyn moved her hand up under his shirt. Lance was pleasantly surprised by her aggression. He welcomed it.

"Come on," she directed with a soft voice. "Let's go to bed."

Lance had often wondered about this eventual moment, and part of him had feared it. He had not been with that many women. Part of him had worried about being able to satisfy Jaelyn. But now, he felt different. Confident.

"All right," he said with a sly grin. He took her hand, and they slinked away to his bedroom.

The young couple made love. Lance was completely in control of his earlier nervousness, somehow knowing exactly what to do and how. They both enjoyed the erotic encounter to the fullest. When they had exhausted their passion, they lay together and fell asleep.

It was after midnight when he heard it.

A smacking sound pulled Lance from his slumber. It was the sound of a horse licking its chops in the dark. *I'm dreaming*, he thought, his mind still foggy from sleep. *About that horse we couldn't see in the graveyard.* He tried to doze off again.

He heard it again, and his eyes snapped open. It sounded like the sticky, flapping lips of a thirsty horse.

Lance quickly raised himself up on his elbows. *What the hell?* he fretted, believing there was an animal with them in the lightless room. His eyes adjusted to the dark, and he scanned the bedroom. Nothing unusual was seen. Just his nightstand, the couple's clothes on the floor, the desk, and Lance's bathrobe draped over a chair.

But something was not right. The robe was positioned higher than the back of the chair. Lance squinted to better focus his sight. The bathrobe was not resting over the chair — it appeared to be *sitting* upright.

The sight jolted Lance. He reached for his phone on

the nightstand and hurriedly activated the flashlight app on its screen. Sure enough, the light showed the cotton bathrobe sitting straight and full as if someone was wearing it, watching him.

Lance got out of bed. Slowly, tentatively, he worked his way toward the shape on the chair. He kept the LED light from his phone aimed squarely at the tan robe. One of the sleeves moved ever so slightly, and then the entire bathrobe suddenly collapsed into an empty heap.

Lance froze in his tracks. After a second of stillness, he resumed crossing the bedroom floor. He arrived at the chair and gripped the robe. He lifted it, revealing a foreign object underneath.

It was an old, dirty claw hammer, and the steel head looked like it was coated in dried blood. Lance noticed some writing on the handle. It was a single word, a name. MOREAU.

"Jesus!" Lance exclaimed, suddenly recognizing the hammer. It was the same one they had borrowed from the motel owner in Colorado, the one they used to break the chest open.

And probably the one that was used to kill the motel owner.

No, no, no, Lance thought. *There's no way I have the murder weapon in my room. It can't be here.* He knew the tool had been left in the motel room before the group checked out three days ago. So how did it end up here?

Jaelyn stirred in the bed, giving a little moan. Lance turned his head in her direction to see if he had woken her. She was still asleep, just repositioning herself. He brought his eyes back to the chair.

The hammer was gone.

Lance's eyes darted around the bedroom, searching for the hammer. It was nowhere to be seen. Lance felt the hot flush of panic, then helpless confusion, and finally disbelief. The puzzling disappearance of the hammer reminded him of the eyeball that had also inexplicably vanished.

Now he questioned whether he had really seen any of it at all.

CHAPTER 14
VISIONS

Jim was burning up, sweating. He lay staring up at the bedroom ceiling and the fan above him in the dark. As sleepy as he was, he could not fall asleep.

Frustrated, he got out of bed and went to the kitchen for a glass of water. He added a few ice cubes to provide the desired chill, swirled the glass, and drank the water down. Then he refilled the glass and took it to the bedroom.

He took another long drink and set the glass on his nightstand. Feeling better, he lay down once more. The scant light from the streetlights reflected off the whirling fan blades. Jim focused on the fan, and it relaxed his mind.

Then he saw teeth.

It was just a brief flash amid the spinning reflection, but it was clear. Jim could swear he had seen an image of gnashing teeth. Shaking the thought, he told himself he was probably teetering on the edge of sleep. He took a long breath and closed his eyes.

Clack. Clack.

Jim heard the distinctive sound of teeth biting together. *No*, he commanded himself, *it's not really there.*

Clack. Clack, clack. The noise continued, tormenting Jim. It grew louder and more frequent. And it sounded like it was getting closer. Unable to ignore his urge to look, Jim opened his eyes.

He saw a mouthful of large teeth in midair, just a few feet above his face.

"Ahhh!" he cried, swiping at the horrible sight with his arm. The image dissipated. "What the hell?" he said, panting. He was still hot. Turning to his side, he reached for the glass on the nightstand.

A set of broad teeth floated above the glass, waiting for his hand.

"Shit!" he blurted, yanking his hand back to the bed. His eyes glued to the vision, he studied it in disbelief. In the meager light, he saw human teeth with no mouth around them. Just — *teeth.* They were suspended in the air, chomping. *Clack, clack.* The mouthful began to drift slowly toward him.

Jim was paralyzed by fear and confusion. How was this happening? He knew his Zuni ancestors were prone to visions, and believed strongly in them, but Jim was not that way. So how on earth was he seeing this?

I'm losing my mind, thought Jim. He shut his eyes and fought to regain control of his mind. *It's not there, it's not there.* He pulled the sheet protectively over him.

Clackclackclackclack.

He could tell the torturous sounds were coming from more than one spot now. Jim opened his eyes again. There were three sets of teeth hovering over him. But they were not human teeth anymore; they were like nothing he had ever seen before. Small and jagged, and a great many of them in each ghastly mouthful. Gnashing and chomping.

Then they began swooping at him.

"Go away!" he yelled desperately. He covered his face with his hands.

The ethereal mouths struck him, biting at him through the sheet. They did not break his skin, but he could definitely feel the painful pinches.

His brain searched for an explanation or an escape. Jim realized this was likely a vision brought about by supernatural forces. He tried to remember everything his people knew about visions.

And how to deal with them.

He thought back on what his grandfather told him. The Zuni knew that some visions were omens of death. Their shamans could call out to spirits in the other plane, and those spirits could be used to force the bad omens away. It was worth a try.

Jim did not have a fetish to use. He had no carvings, talismans, or charms that held the powers of spirit animals. At this point, all he could do was meditate. He drew a long, disciplined breath and tried to force out everything around him. Jim's grandfather once taught him how to meditate and how to reach out to the beyond. Jim silently called out to his ancestors for assistance, stretching his mind and projecting himself. He also concentrated on the spirits of the bear and the eagle for strength and luck.

After what seemed like an eternity, the visions ceased,

and Jim was finally able to calm himself to sleep.

CHAPTER 15
THE ALPHA MALE

Lance woke feeling woozy, so much that he thought he was ill. Concerned, he forced himself from the mattress and to his feet. Walking to the bathroom was an arduous task; this was the weakest Lance had ever felt in his life.

He looked at his reflection in the mirror. His face was pale. But he was okay last night. And if he was sick, he would feel a fever, aching, or some other kind of distinguishable discomfort. None of those symptoms were his, however; he just felt tired. *What's wrong with me?* he pondered. He leaned closer and studied his glassy eyes.

Lance felt a sudden twinge in the side of his neck. It was not painful, but it got his attention. He closed his eyes and rubbed the spot.

At once, he felt fine. When he opened his eyes, Lance found himself staring at the face of someone healthy and energetic. His weakened condition seemed to have vanished. He felt rejuvenated, like a new man.

"That's weird," he muttered, removing his hand from his neck. Oh well, he figured, he must have found one of the many pressure points in his body that are known to acupuncturists. He sauntered to the kitchen to make his morning coffee.

He saw his roommate already pouring water into the coffee maker. David acknowledged Lance with a bob of his head. "What's up?"

"Mornin'," Lance replied.

"Coffee will be ready in just a few minutes." David faced his roommate. "So...," he began, just about to ask how Lance's evening with Jaelyn went.

Lance's bedroom door opened, and Jaelyn shuffled out. "Hey guys," she said softly.

"Hey," they responded in unison.

"What time is it?" she asked, yawning.

David glanced at the clock on the microwave. "Nine-thirty," he said.

Jaelyn's head was a little foggy from last night's wine. "I need some water," she stated, walking toward the cupboard. She pulled a glass from the shelf and stopped on her way to the sink to give Lance a tender kiss.

David could not help but smile at the sight. He was happy to see that the couple had spent the night together. They had taken their relationship to the next level. And David liked that. He thought Jaelyn was a nice match for his friend and vice versa. The two were good for each other.

The trio was soon drinking coffee on the couch. The TV was on, its dull morning shows providing the comfort of background noise.

Jaelyn turned to David. "How did your date go?" she enquired, knowing about the plans Karen had made with him.

The Latino grinned innocently. "Fine," was all he said.

"Whatever," said Jaelyn, laughing. "I'm sure it went better than that." She continued prodding. "So?"

"So what?"

"Did you two do it?"

"A gentleman never tells," said David.

Jaelyn jumped on the set-up. "Ha! In that case, you can totally tell us!"

Lance chuckled at the jibing of his roommate. "Indeed."

David's appearance could not conceal how his evening went. The bags under his eyes indicated he had been up all night, and his short hair was smashed in every direction. And there was a contentment about him. But he feared spilling the beans about his night with Karen in front of her sorority sister. Word would get back to Karen; he had to play it cool.

"I could just as easily ask how your night together went," said David.

Jaelyn's mouth curled into a grin. "It went the same as yours," she revealed.

David raised his coffee cup. "Cheers, then."

They resumed drinking their coffee while watching nothing in particular on TV. After a while, the group was awake enough to be hungry. "I think I'll nuke some burritos," said David, getting up. "You guys want one?"

Jaelyn wrinkled her nose. "Not really. I want to go out for a cheesesteak."

Lance was on board with that. "Sounds good," he said.

"I'll do that with you. Just let me get a shower first."

"Me too," she said. "I've got to go home to shower and change. How about we meet up at Hoagy's around one?"

"Works for me," said Lance.

Jaelyn gathered her things and kissed Lance. Then she left the apartment to go home and get ready.

***

When it was time to head out, Lance walked across Apache Boulevard and made his way through the campus. He was passing by Memorial Union when he heard someone call his name. Looking up, Lance spotted his classmate Deshawn coming out of Hayden Library.

Deshawn, a devout Christian, was the student who had recently been helping Lance find his faith. Through discussions of creation, intelligent design, and historical documentation, Deshawn had opened Lance's eyes — and heart — to the world of Christianity. It connected with Lance. It had made him a happier, better person.

At this moment, however, the sight of Deshawn made Lance feel surprisingly uncomfortable. He stopped in his tracks while his friend approached.

"Hey, Lance," the young man said, adding a fist bump to his greeting. "How's it going?"

"Pretty good," replied Lance. He was hesitant to converse with Deshawn for some unknown reason.

"Are you ready for classes to start?"

"I suppose."

"Hey, don't forget," said Deshawn. "We're still gonna do Bible study every Wednesday night if you want to join us."

Don't listen to that shit, said something deep inside

Lance. *Ignore that nonsense.*

Lance was ashamed of the thought in his head. "I might just do that," he said to put his conscience back on track.

"Cool. So you get all registered okay?"

Lance nodded. "I did." He suddenly noticed a slight pressure around his eyes. His vision clouded ever so slightly. Now all he wanted to do was get away from Deshawn. "Hey, listen," Lance said politely. "I'm running late for lunch with my girlfriend. So I'll catch you sometime later?"

Deshawn understood completely. "Say no more, my friend, have a nice lunch, and I'll see you around." With a pleasant wave, he continued on his merry way.

Lance arrived at Hoagy's, a sandwich restaurant with outdoor seating. He saw that Jaelyn was not there yet, so he stood by the entrance and waited. Only a few minutes went by before she appeared. Her hair pulled back in a ponytail, she caught sight of him and quickened her pace to join him at the entrance.

The couple went inside, and the smells from the grill made their mouths water. They ordered large cheesesteak sandwiches with peppers and onions, sides of hot, fresh fries, and sodas. Then they found a table outside on the patio, where they sat and waited for their food.

A few minutes later, their lunch was brought out to them. The famished pair dug into their feast with enthusiasm. The steak sandwiches were just what they needed. Coming here for lunch was a good call.

"Hey, Jaelyn!" said a man's voice.

The couple looked up and saw Todd Ryan weaving around the tables to get closer.

Lance turned his back to the unwelcome visitor. He had always been intimidated by the larger, athletic man, especially knowing he was attracted to Jaelyn.

"How's it going?" the chipper blond smiled.

"Good," said Jaelyn. "Just having some lunch."

"You should let me take you to lunch sometime," Todd suggested, watching Lance through the corner of his eye. "Or better yet, I'll take you to a nice dinner."

"Come on, Todd," griped Jaelyn, clearly annoyed. "We've talked about this before."

"We've had some fun together," Todd argued. "We should hang out again."

"Sorry, Todd, I'm not interested. I'm with Lance, as you can see."

Lance added his contribution. "And, as you can see, we're trying to enjoy our lunch." His comment was just loud enough to attract the attention of others at nearby tables.

Todd noticed the extra eyes on him. He puffed up. "Listen, buddy," he said. "I'm trying to have a conversation with my friend here. So how about you keep your mouth shut, you rude little shit?"

Something inside Lance awakened. Something bold, unafraid. He stood from his chair and placed himself in front of the frat boy. "Is there something you need help with, son?"

Jaelyn's eyes widened a bit. She appreciated the gesture but knew Lance was taking on much more than he could handle. "Lance...," she began.

Lance flattened his hand behind him, signaling to Jaelyn that he had the situation under control.

Todd moved closer to Lance. "I'm not the one that's

gonna need help here," he smirked. "Now get out of my way and let me talk to the lady."

Lance stood still, unyielding. "Go on now. She obviously doesn't want to talk to you," he said assertively. His voice was so firm that it almost sounded like someone else's.

Todd had put up with this display for long enough. He had to show this little man who was in charge. He launched his arms forcefully in an attempt to shove Lance in the chest. Lance reacted instantly. With one hand, he effortlessly pushed Todd's hands aside before they could make contact. Todd spun around and stumbled, just barely regaining his balance.

Jaelyn tensed at the exchange. "Stop it!"

The two men ignored her request. Lance was completely rigid, his feet firm where he stood. Todd was stunned by Lance's ability to counter him. He gawked at Lance.

There was something odd about Lance's stare, like a cold, black fire pushing through from behind his eyes. It was something Todd realized he wanted nothing to do with. It terrified him.

Keeping his eyes locked with Lance's, Todd slowly stepped backward. He did not speak a word. He just nodded peaceably and walked away.

"What the hell...?" Jaelyn finally said. "Jesus, Lance, you could've gotten hurt." She looked at him, standing still with his back to her. He did not respond. "Lance," she said. "Hey, are you okay?"

Lance finally turned around. "Yeah," he stated with a reassuring smile. "I'm fine." He returned to his seat and took a bite of his sandwich.

She touched his hand. "Thank you for getting rid of him, but you really had me worried. I don't want you hurt." Then she sat up straighter. "How the hell did you do that?"

He shrugged. "Just reflexes."

"Well, you've got some killer reflexes, then," said Jaelyn. "But it's not just that. You stared him down to a frightened pup."

"Eh."

"Seriously, how did you do that?"

"He was bothering us," Lance said matter-of-factly.

"Well, thank you again. That guy is like a zit that won't go away."

Lance slowly turned his head to face her. "Don't worry. I don't believe he'll be bothering you anymore."

Jaelyn gazed at him with adoring eyes. Then she continued eating her lunch. There was a proud grin on her face, although she tried to suppress it. Her boyfriend had impressed her. He'd stood up for her and gotten rid of a situation that she thought would not end well. Pride was brimming inside her.

***

That evening the gang decided to get together at one of the bars near the campus. They met at Devils' Tavern, its name and logo incorporating the university's Sun Devils moniker. It was one of the more popular bars around, being large enough for many patrons to gather and still be able to hear each other.

The bar was pretty full for a Thursday night. The clientele consisted mostly of students enjoying the end of their summer break. Lance and his friends worked their way to the bar. Jaelyn and Karen were in the mood for margaritas while the three men ordered bottles of beer. With drinks in hand, the crew found an open table and sat down to drink.

The hot topic of the evening was Lance's confrontation with the frat boy. Jaelyn excitedly delivered her account of what had happened.

Karen's face froze. "Todd? You mean…?"

Jaelyn nodded. "Yep, *that* Todd."

Jim sat up straight and crossed his arms, beaming. "Way to go, Bowser."

"Dude, you were a *king* today!" David said excitedly. "That's so awesome."

"I don't know what happened," Lance admitted. "Honestly, everything just *happened*. I didn't even think about anything I was doing."

"Well, whatever you were thinking," said Jaelyn, "I'm just glad you didn't get hurt." A smile crept up the side of her mouth. "And I'm so glad you put him in his place."

"Me too." Lance swallowed the rest of his beer. He got up to get another bottle. "Anybody else?"

"Yeah," said David and Jim together.

Lance walked to the bar and ordered three more bottles. While he was waiting, he felt a slight twinge in the side of his neck. He barely noticed it, unknowingly reaching up to touch it.

He gathered the beers and brought them to their table. He passed one to Jim and one to David. Then he twisted the cap off his own bottle.

Jim raised his bottled beer and said, "*Banzai!*" expecting Lance's usual reply of "*Kanpai.*"

Lance hoisted his bottle and merely said, "Cheers." Then he knocked back the entire beer.

CHAPTER 16
BLOODY DREAMS

It was one in the morning before the group was finished drinking in the bar. Feeling sufficiently impaired, they deemed it time to call it a night. They settled their tab at the bar.

Outside, Lance and Jaelyn gave each other a long goodnight kiss. David and Karen kissed as well. Jim stood patiently while the couples parted. Then Jaelyn and Karen headed across campus to their sorority house while the men staggered toward their apartment complex.

Once they arrived home, the men stopped at their respective doors to unlock them. "You sure you don't want to stay up for another beer?" Lance asked David.

His roommate shook his head emphatically. "No, no, I'm good. I need a tall glass of water, some aspirin, and my pillow."

Lance looked over to Jim. "How about you, Jim? Up for some more drinking?"

Jim thought for a moment, but not about consuming more alcohol. He was trying to come up with a funny response regarding his being an Indian, not necessarily meaning he was always up for drinking. But fatigue and inebriation were too much for his wit to conquer. "Naw," he replied. "I'm gonna hit the sheets before my head starts spinning."

"Fine," Lance succumbed. He was probably tired himself, though he definitely felt a little energy still inside him. "Catch you tomorrow."

"Yeah," said David. "Goodnight, 'Sleeps With Sheep.'" He opened the door, and Lance followed him inside the apartment.

David got ready for bed and turned in. Lance stayed up for a bit, watching some quiet TV until he felt sleepy enough to go to bed. Finally, Lance's eyelids grew heavy. At two-thirty, he dragged himself to his bedroom and collapsed onto the mattress.

At one point, he began to dream.

He was in a bedroom, but it was not his own. And someone else was standing there in the dark with him. A figure was leaning over somebody's bed. Its familiar silhouette was recognizable.

It was Jack Grainger.

Lance was helpless to say anything or to even move. All he could do was watch. Grainger knew Lance was there but did not seem to think anything of it. He ignored Lance's presence and focused on the sleeping person before him.

Straining his eyes, Lance could see that the person in bed was Todd Ryan. *What am I doing in the frat boy's room?* he mused worriedly. *And what if he wakes up?*

As if in response to Lance's mental query, Grainger drew his index finger and poked the sleeping man's chest. Todd stirred, opened his eyes, and saw the figure above him. As the shocked student sucked a quick breath to react, Grainger took the butt of a large knife and struck Todd on the forehead. The frat boy was knocked unconscious.

Lance stared in awe at how easily Grainger had subdued his target. His awe turned into confusion when he saw the silhouette remove the clothing from Todd's body. Then he watched the dark shape collect some of the shirts from a pile of dirty clothes and use them to bind his naked victim to the bedposts.

A part of him was enjoying this. Todd Ryan was getting a little payback, which pleased Lance. But that amusement quickly turned into horror when he saw the shape take the blade of the knife and cut a slice down Todd's center.

Powerless to move, Lance watched while the silhouette cut Todd's skin into sections. The intruder then proceeded to pull each section apart from the muscle tissue beneath. Mortified, Lance found himself riveted to the sight of Grainger skinning his victim.

Blood seeped everywhere. The excruciating pain was enough to yank Todd back to consciousness. Before he could scream, Grainger's hand landed forcefully over the frat boy's mouth. He then eliminated the threat of screaming by carving Todd's throat wide open.

Within seconds the subject was lifeless, and Grainger was free to continue flaying the body without distraction. He took the sections of skin and flung them callously to the floor. Lance's eyes took in the horrific event, noting every glistening fiber of the exposed tissue.

Now Lance found himself watching the act from the assailant's point of view. He could feel his arms move exactly the way he saw Grainger's move. He had a sick feeling that he had become Jack Grainger.

Lance woke with a start. His eyes darted around the darkness of his bedroom. His heart was fueled by adrenaline from the disturbing dream. He had to take a slow breath to normalize his pulse.

Trying to flush the terrible dream from his memory, he closed his eyes and made himself go back to sleep.

CHAPTER 17
SHOCKING NEWS

A knocking on the door rattled Lance awake. He opened his eyes and gazed around the bedroom. It was bright with unwanted sunlight. Snarling, he looked at the bedroom window. The blinds were raised, exposing a half-open window.

"What?" he called to the person on the other side of the door.

"Hey man, it's noon," said David. "I was just checking on you to see if you're okay."

"Noon?" Lance checked the clock on the nightstand. "Damn, so it is."

"Want some coffee?"

"Hell yeah," Lance replied. "I'll be right out."

Glancing at the window, he scratched his scalp. *When did I open the window?* he pondered. It was warm in his room last night, but he did not remember wandering to the window to open it. And he certainly would not have needed to raise the blinds to let the night air in. *Whatever, it doesn't matter.*

Lance ambled to the window and closed it. It would be too hot outside during the day to let the late summer air into his bedroom. Then he lowered the blinds and twisted them shut. His window secure, Lance exited the bedroom and joined his roommate in the living area.

"Jesus," said David, "you look like hammered shit."

"Thank you very much," Lance replied with his best Elvis Presley impersonation. He poured himself some coffee and sat on the couch with his friend. "You don't look so hot yourself."

David shooed the air. "Just a little hungover, but I feel okay." He studied his roommate with concern. Lance had been in bed for half the day, yet he still looked like he had been up all night. "There's still some leftover mac and cheese in the fridge if you want."

The food sounded quite appealing to Lance. "God, yes, that actually sounds good." He jumped up from the couch and marched back to the kitchen. He scooped the grub onto a plate and tossed it in the microwave oven. While his cheesy pasta was being reheated, he topped off his coffee cup. Then he brought his fare back to the couch and started eating.

David flipped through the channels to find something enjoyable to watch. He settled on a broadcast of an older superhero movie and set the remote down. The two young men focused on the visual spectacle of mindless entertainment while they sat inert and content.

Suddenly the movie was interrupted by a local news bulletin. The station cut to a shot of one of the afternoon anchors seated behind the newsdesk.

"Good afternoon, I'm Alicia Reedy," said the familiar newscaster, with a grave expression on her face. "We're coming to you live to report breaking news from the ASU campus in Tempe."

Lance and David leaned forward, their ears perking. "Here?" said David. "Shit, I hope it's not a shooter nearby."

Lance doubted it. "Naw, you worry too much."

The newscaster shifted uncomfortably at the desk. "A student was found dead late this morning, in his bedroom at the Beta Theta Pi house, just off campus. Details are still coming in, and Jennifer Williams is on the scene."

The broadcast cut to one of the regular reporters standing in front of the fraternity house. "Thanks, Alicia. I've just spoken to the officers at the scene here, at the Beta Theta Pi house, and they have informed me that one of the students was killed here sometime late last night. There are no leads at the moment, and the police are advising that all students take extra care to keep their doors and windows locked. They also advise students to stay in trusted groups if they have to go out around the campus at night. Obviously, these precautions go for everyone in Tempe until the police can apprehend whoever is responsible. The investigation is ongoing, and I'll report back as we get more information."

"See?" said Lance. "No shooter."

Ten minutes later, Lance's phone rang. Seeing it was Jaelyn calling, he picked up. "Hello," he greeted.

"Lance, oh my God, did you see the news?" she said vigorously.

"Yeah, about a student found dead."

"Not just dead," said Jaelyn, "but slaughtered. And it

was Todd!"

"What?"

"Jesus, Lance, it's terrible! I just talked to Jessica, who's dating Todd's friend Brian, and she told me Todd was found *skinned* – like an animal! She said there was blood all over the bedroom, and the smell was just awful."

Lance tensed. "Shit...," he mumbled. He could not help but think of the horrible dream he'd had. For God's sake, he *saw* Todd being flayed on the bed! His eyes zipped back and forth nervously, unconsciously scanning the living room. He was utterly alarmed, utterly confused. Could he have had something to do with Todd's death? No, that was ridiculous. It was only a nightmare.

"Holy crap, Jaelyn," Lance began, about to tell her about his disturbing dream. But then his senses warned him not to divulge that information. He decided to keep it to himself. He redirected his sentence. "That's messed up."

"Yeah," she replied. There was noticeable panic in her voice. "What are we gonna do, knowing there's a maniac on the campus?"

Lance tried to replace the dread with logic. "Well, like the news said, we'll just make sure to check the locks on our doors and windows so nobody can get inside. And when we go out, we'll stay together. Safety in numbers. Nobody would attack a group of people."

"I suppose," said Jaelyn, some calm returning to her voice. "But God, Lance. To be skinned.... I can't even imagine."

"Try not to think about it," he said. "Seriously, it'll just make you crazy. I mean, I feel sorry for Todd and all—even though he was a dick—but you have to try to not let it get to you. I don't know what else to say."

David's jaw fell open at the mention of Todd's name. "It was *Todd* that died?" he whispered, and Lance nodded. "Wow, man."

Lance imagined Jaelyn and Karen were quite shaken by the news of a murder so close to their own house. "Do you need us to come over?" he asked.

Jaelyn hesitated before answering, and Lance thought he heard her sniffling. "Yes," she admitted. "I need to see you."

"It's all right, sweetie," assured Lance, standing up. "We're coming over. Be there soon, okay?"

"Okay," Jaelyn acknowledged. "Hurry."

Lance said goodbye and ended the call. He brought his eyes up to his roommate. "Holy shit, dude. The frat boy dick is dead, and whoever killed him skinned him."

David thought he had heard wrong. "I'm sorry, what?"

"Yep, just like in *Predator*."

David recalled the ghastly images from the movie, and he cringed. "Damn."

"The girls are pretty freaked out. They want us to come over."

The Latino strained to get up from the couch. "Duty calls, I suppose."

David took the first shower. When he vacated the bathroom to dress, Lance stepped into the shower stall. After a hot shower to wash and invigorate him, Lance migrated to his bedroom.

He searched the floor for a minute and frowned. The clothes he had worn last night were nowhere to be found.

Luckily, he found the contents of his jeans placed on the desk. At least he had not lost his wallet and keys along with his clothing.

Lance dressed, stuffed his pockets with the items on the desk, and returned to the bathroom. He ran a comb through his hair, parting it on its regular left side. Then he was ready to lock up and leave with his roommate.

Walking east alongside Apache Boulevard, David prodded Lance for more information. "So, like, who found the body?"

"I don't know," said Lance. "All Jaelyn told me was that one of his friends told one of her friends that he was found skinned and that there was blood everywhere."

"Was his skin left there, or did someone take it?"

"I don't know," Lance repeated. "We'll find out more when we get there."

David shook his head in disbelief. "Dude, that's so fucked up. We might have a serial killer here on campus with us."

They arrived at the sorority house and rang the doorbell. Jaelyn opened the door and let them inside. Then she led them to the living room where Karen was sitting. Karen's light-blue eyes sparkled a little brighter when she saw David. She stood up to welcome him with a hug.

"Hey, you," he said, giving her a light kiss on the forehead. "Crazy stuff, huh?"

"Terrifying," she replied. "My God, David, who could *do* something like that to someone?"

"I don't know, Karen. I can't even begin to comprehend that level of sickness." He brought his hand up her back and gently rubbed her trapezius muscles. "I'm just glad nothing happened to any of you girls."

"Amen," said Lance. He surveyed the room around him, seeing some of the other sorority sisters moving about. They seemed restless, nervous. There was a gloomy vibe in the house. "What do you say we get out of here?" he suggested. "I think a nice walk in the sun would cheer us up a little."

The idea was agreeable to the rest of the group. "Yeah," said Jaelyn, "I don't want to be cooped up in here today."

"Have you eaten yet?" Lance asked, and the girls shook their heads. "Let's go find someplace where we can all get some grub and sit."

Despite the gruesome images of Todd's death on their minds, the women could not ignore the pangs from their empty stomachs. The group left the house and walked along Rural Road, deciding what they were hungry for. They agreed on going to The Halal Guys for gyro platters.

They brought their meals to a table and ate their late lunch of chicken and beef. While scooping some hummus with her pita bread, Karen pulled her phone out. She briefly checked her emails and messages.

"Jim's looking for us," Karen announced.

"His door was closed when we left," said David, "so we figured he was sleeping."

"You all want to come back to our place after we eat?" Lance offered. "We can hang out with Jim and do something." The others shrugged and nodded, having no better plans for the day.

After their lunch, the crew walked to the apartment building. They climbed the concrete stairs to Lance's second-story unit. Jim was waiting for them next door, leaning on the metal railing.

"Whatcha all up to today?" he asked.

"Just walking around," said David, "having some lunch."

Jim shielded his eyes and looked up toward the sun. "It's a hot day for walking around."

"Tell me about it," said Jaelyn. "Let's go inside and cool down for a bit."

They entered Lance and David's apartment and found seats in the living area. David turned the TV on. "Did you hear about Todd?" he asked Jim.

"I heard someone died," said Jim. "Was it that Todd guy?"

"Yep," said David. "Someone killed him. And not only that, but they skinned him."

Jim's eyes popped. "Ed Gein, party of two!" he joked. "I'll bet the pretty boy doesn't look so good anymore."

"You look a little ragged yourself," Lance noted.

"I haven't been sleeping," admitted Jim. "Nightmares about teeth."

Karen cringed a little. "Teeth?"

"Yeah, just a bunch of teeth biting at me."

"You need to lay off the peyote, Jim," said David.

The day went by pleasantly. The group spent some time outdoors playing Frisbee golf. It was always a fun daytime excursion for them. After a couple of hours of being in the late-summer sun, the crew wanted to go somewhere for dinner.

They went to a Mexican grill for oversized burritos.

After going through the line and building their meals, they brought their food to a table in the middle of the restaurant. They dug into their feast with voracious appetites. While eating, the group talked about how they were dreading the upcoming semester. But they lightened the mood by discussing the fun things they had done during the summer break.

"The ghost lights were the best," Karen claimed. "That was super cool."

"It was," agreed Jim. "I was skeptical, I'll admit, but they were awesome to see."

Karen brought her phone out of her pocket. "I've got some great pictures from that trip. Check 'em out." She pulled up her cache of photos and found the ones from that weekend. The group huddled around her and looked while she scrolled through each photo. They saw pictures of the rustic mining town, the motel they had stayed in, and many of the cemetery and the field.

"Aw, look at that one," said Jaelyn. Karen had advanced to the pictures of their visit to the abandoned mine, and there was a shot of Jaelyn and Lance smiling together.

"What's that?" said David, leaning closer to the screen.

"What?" Karen said.

"Right above Lance." He was pointing to what appeared to be a dark, cloudy figure looming behind Lance.

The others noticed it now. "Whoa," said Jim, "what the hell is that?"

Lance studied the shadow attached to him in the photo. It was subtle, not pronounced at all, but looked like the ghostly shape of a man crowding Lance's space. "Aw, that's nothing," he concluded. "Just some kind of bizarre double image caused by the sun."

"What a crazy trip that was," commented Jaelyn. "Those ghost lights dancing in the field, that's something I'll never forget. And the bugs that came out of that chest, holy shit! I still can't comprehend what happened to them!"

"You still have that wooden chest, right?" Karen asked Lance.

He nodded. "Yep. In my bedroom."

"I'd like to get online and do some research on it. Would you mind if I borrowed it?"

"Not at all," said Lance. "After dinner, we can go back to my place, and you can grab it."

The crew returned to the apartment after their meal as the sun was starting to settle behind the Arizona landscape. They went inside and got some beers from the refrigerator. While the students started drinking, Karen reminded Lance that she wanted the old chest. He stood to get it from his bedroom.

Lance felt that slight twinge in the side of his neck again. He stopped in his tracks, then turned to Karen. "It's in my room there," he said, "on my desk."

David felt an odd change in Lance's voice. He looked at his roommate curiously. It was almost as if Lance did not want to bring the chest to her.

Karen walked into Lance's bedroom. She came out a moment later with the wooden chest in her hands. The rest of the group recognized the distinct box, its wood practically blackened from being buried in the earth for so many years. The illegible carvings on the lid were highly visible in the apartment's light.

"You sure you don't mind me borrowing this for a while?" Karen checked.

"Nope," said Lance. "You can keep it, for all I care."

Karen was shocked by this generous statement but was grateful to hear it. "Thanks, Lance. But I'll get it back to you when I'm done checking up on it. After all, you are the one who found it."

"Naw, you keep it."

David was taken aback by his friend's willingness to let go of the historic relic. He would have assumed Lance would want to keep the excavated souvenir; it may have been valuable. But David kept his thoughts to himself. It was Lance's decision.

Jim proposed a different topic of discussion. "You can read up on the history of that thing tomorrow," he said. "I say we figure out what we all want to do tonight."

"I say we cruise Mill Avenue and party," suggested Lance.

Mill Avenue was the hot spot of the ASU campus and would be kicking tonight. It was Friday, after all, the start of a festive weekend. The crew was good with the idea of roaming Mill Avenue with the rest of the drunken mob there.

Even Jim, who had not been sleeping well the past few nights, figured he could use the festive distraction. He stood up, ready to go. "Sounds like a plan, *kemosabe*. Let's do it."

"Yeah?" Lance said, scanning everybody's faces to see that they agreed.

"Yeah," David nodded enthusiastically.

"All right," said Lance. He grabbed his keys and moved

toward the door.

"Don't you want to use the bathroom first?" asked Jaelyn, reminding Lance of his usual bathroom visit to appease his irritable bowel before going anywhere.

"No, what for?"

"You know," she said, lowering her voice. "For your IBS?"

Lance seemed oblivious to what she was saying. "What do you mean?"

She leaned closer. "Um, your irritable bowel? Hello?"

He laughed. "My bowels are fine," he scoffed. "Now come on," he added, surveying the group of surprised faces. "Let's go find us a party."

CHAPTER 18
THE CURSED CHEST

Karen stirred in her bed the following morning. Her head was throbbing, and she felt nauseous. "Ohhhhh," she groaned, covering her head with her arm. The headache was going to make her sick. She needed to sit up.

Last night replayed through her mind. The group had blended with a large group of students that were wandering Mill Avenue, visiting bar after bar. She could not remember the last time she drank so much. It would not have been so bad if Lance had not insisted that they kept drinking so late. The women did not get home until two in the morning.

It was a miracle Karen had not thrown up. Her sour stomach was still contemplating the idea, and Karen had to keep that from happening. Seeing an empty glass on her desk, she rose from the bed and grabbed it. She hurried to the bathroom down the hall and filled the glass with cold water. Drinking the pure liquid seemed to soothe her stomach and quell her urge to vomit.

She returned to her room and to her bed. Walking had made her head pound even more. Needing something else to focus on, Karen reached for the remote on the nightstand and turned her TV on. She just wanted to lie still and watch some droll Saturday morning programming.

There was a quiet knock on her door. "Come in," she croaked.

Jaelyn opened the door and entered the bedroom. "Hey," she said. "How're you feeling?"

Karen looked at her with obvious pain. "I'm sooooooo hung over," she whined. "Everything hurts. Especially my head. And when I walk around, it just gets worse."

"Oh baby, I'm sorry. I was going to see if you wanted to come to get something to eat with me."

"Ugh. No, I'm a wreck. I'm afraid I'm gonna have to just stay in bed all day and try to heal."

"You poor thing," said Jaelyn. "Although I understand. I'm lucky I don't feel worse than I already do. We drank *way* too much last night."

"Your crazy boyfriend certainly didn't help," Karen pointed out. "I've never seen him like that before."

Jaelyn shook her head. "Me neither. I don't know where all that energy came from. I'll bet he's hurting this morning too."

Karen placed her hands over her aching head. "Good," she said half-jokingly. "Serves him right."

"I know just what you need," Jaelyn stated. "I'm going to drive to French Fry Heaven. You need some poutine; it's the perfect hangover food."

As damaged as Karen felt, the suggestion of cheese

curds and brown gravy over hot fries appealed to her stomach. "That would be awesome," she said, reaching for her purse. "Take my card."

"I gotcha," said Jaelyn, happy to pay for both of them. "You can get the next one." She started to leave.

"Oh, hey," said Karen, as the thought struck her. "If you're swinging by the boys' place, wanna grab that old chest for me? I think I left it in their living room. It would give me something to do today."

"Sure," Jaelyn smiled. "See you in a little bit."

Karen spent the better part of an hour lying peacefully in the bed. She watched a documentary about the ecosystem of some lonely island in the South Pacific, narrated by a man with a soft, quiet, soothing voice. Her attention on the show, the headache dissipated a little.

Jaelyn returned with a bag of food. Karen could smell the rich aroma as soon as her sorority sister entered the room. Her mouth was watering for the fatty hangover food.

"Oh my God, that smells so good," Karen remarked. She sat up and propped her pillows behind her.

Jaelyn opened the bag and produced a Styrofoam platter. "Here you go, just what the doctor ordered." She handed Karen the promised fries, riddled with cheese curds and slathered in brown gravy.

"You are so awesome, thank you."

"No problem," said Jaelyn. "Oh, and here's that chest for you to study." She showed Karen the artifact she'd brought over from Lance's place. "Where do you want it?"

Karen motioned toward her desk. "Over there is fine, next to the computer."

Jaelyn set the weathered box on the corner for her friend to research. Then she sat in the chair and opened her own container to start eating the gluttonous order of smothered fries. The young women enjoyed the flavorful fare while commenting on some of the events and conversations from the night before.

Karen ate half of her order before closing the Styrofoam cover. "I'll have to eat the rest later," she admitted. "But it'll happen—I have all day."

Jaelyn chuckled. "I have no doubt." She had already finished her meal and figured it was time to give Karen some privacy so she could rest and feel better. "I'm gonna go chill out in my room. If you need anything, come get me?"

"Will do," said Karen. "And thank you again for getting food. You're the greatest."

"My pleasure, sweetie," Jaelyn replied. "I'll see you later." She got up and left Karen's room, closing the door behind her.

Karen lay back and focused on the TV. She watched for about ten minutes before her phone rang. Looking at the display, she saw David was calling. Willing to talk to him, she picked up and said hello.

"Hey you," said David. "What's up?"

"Not me," Karen declared. "I'm paying the price for staying out as late as we did last night."

"Me too. I can't believe we lasted that long."

"Yeah, my body's gonna be on the mend today."

"Want to do something together tonight?" he asked, eager to see her again. "Just the two of us?"

"I do," she said, "but I feel like total crap today. I need

to stay in and recover. I'm sorry."

"Yeah," David confessed, "we did drink an insane amount."

"And it hit me like a truck."

"I'm sorry you don't feel good. Hope you get rested up."

"Thank you, I will. And when I'm back to normal, we'll do something."

"Definitely. I'd like to get together again," said David.

Karen smiled. "Me too. How about tomorrow night?"

"Sounds like a plan," David accepted. He would have to wait another day before seeing her again, but he understood staying home to battle a bad hangover. "Binge watch a show or something, and make sure you eat."

"Okay, Doc," said Karen. "Jaelyn brought me some food. I'm good to go."

"Alrighty then," David said. "I guess I'll talk to you tomorrow?"

"Until then," she said sweetly. "'Bye." She ended the call and set the phone down.

Karen spent the next hour watching one of her regular shows. Her headache slowly subsided, and her eyelids grew heavy. She allowed herself to fall asleep and take a restful nap.

At some point in the afternoon, she woke again. Needing to pee, she slid out of bed and made her way to the bathroom. She felt much better than she did earlier. Having eaten some food to placate her system and sleeping a few more hours to subdue her hangover, Karen was almost back to normal. She relieved herself and drank some more water, then went back to her room.

Karen heard voices on the lawn below her window. Peering out, she saw her sorority sisters leaving. They were likely going to a movie together, their Saturday matinee ritual. She was a little sad that they were all going without her. But she was okay with staying home alone to just relax and heal.

Karen brought her eyes to the wooden chest. The size of a car battery, it took up the entire corner of her desk. She recalled the incident in the Colorado motel room when the army of palmetto bugs had spilled out, mortifying the group. For a moment, she feared something like that would happen again. But she was in the familiar comfort of her own room, nowhere near the remote mining town. This was her turf.

And this would be the perfect time for her to get online and dig up some information about the history surrounding that old chest.

Setting the container of leftover fries next to her keyboard, she sat at the desk and awakened her computer. When she was successfully logged onto the Internet, she typed "Black Jack Silver Valley" in the search box. The search engine compiled an endless list of links that it deemed applicable.

Karen was stunned by what she saw. The man whose name she had been told about was apparently quite a notorious character. She saw articles describing his history, his crimes, and how mercilessly he had killed his victims.

"Jesus," she said. "This guy was a monster."

She typed the words "Jack Grainger chest" to specify what she was searching for. Rolling down the screen, she spotted something about a wooden chest and Grainger's remains. Karen clicked on the link to open the article.

She read about Jack Grainger murdering a black prospector from Louisiana in 1882. This act prompted the man's sister to ride to Colorado to determine what had happened. The woman's name was Estelle Toutant, and she traveled with her two sons. It did not take long for Estelle to learn who was responsible and track the murderer down.

Reading on, Karen saw a passage describing what happened next. According to the testimony of anonymous eyewitnesses, Estelle and her sons bound Grainger to a table and killed him. Then she burned his body and deposited the ashes of certain remains inside what they called a "soul chest." After that, the wooden box and the rest of Grainger's body were buried together in a field near Silver Valley.

Now Karen was engrossed in the story. She began a new search, looking for the history of Estelle Toutant. What she found was fascinating.

Estelle was allegedly a powerful voodoo priestess, or mambo, in Haiti. She eventually left her island birthplace and sailed to America with her younger brother Emmanuel Charbronne. Settling in the French Quarter of Louisiana, Estelle continued to practice her Haitian magic. She married Samuel Toutant, a Creole of color, who made his living as both a cook and a musician. They had two children together, James and Joseph before Samuel died of pneumonia. Estelle's brother Emmanuel helped her raise the boys.

Emmanuel, following the lure of gold and silver, left Louisiana in 1880 and headed west to prospect. He had been away for two years when Estelle received word that her brother had been brutally murdered. He had suffered an agonizing death from being tortured and skinned. Armed with rage and her teenage sons, Estelle went to Colorado to visit Emmanuel's grave and avenge him.

Rumor had it that Estelle used voodoo magic to find the killer. She was led to Jack Grainger, who was still staying in the town where Emmanuel died. After that, it was unclear what actually happened. Legends suggested that Estelle killed Grainger, burned his body, cursed the remains, and condemned his soul to a small walnut box. Whatever the case, Jack Grainger was confirmed to be dead and buried in Silver Valley.

Karen thought she saw movement out of the corner of her eye. She focused on the old chest resting on the desk. It was almost black from being buried in the earth for so many years. Karen's focus was drawn to the illegible carvings on its lid. The writing was something she could not read, something foreign. Perhaps the markings were part of the voodoo curse put there by Estelle Toutant.

Karen's fascination with the chest was now cresting. The relic she had just read about had a remarkable history, and she had it right in front of her. Wanting to study it further, she set her hands on the loose lid and lifted it away.

The chest was once again packed with quivering insects — the same mysterious palmetto bugs that she and her friends saw back in Colorado. She lurched back in her chair upon seeing them.

The bugs suddenly erupted from the wooden chest. An army of them gushed out in a seemingly endless flow. They spilled out across the desk, down to the floor, and began to fill the room. Karen jumped up and stood on her chair, shrieking as the scuttling, reddish-brown army surrounded her.

Then the insects came directly at her. They rushed up the chair legs and onto her body. Screaming, Karen swept them off as quickly as she could. But there were far too many. The palmetto bugs swarmed and covered her. Within seconds she felt the poking of their tiny legs on her face. She closed her eyes tightly, continuing to brush them off. Then she had to force her mouth shut as the bugs tried to enter it.

Karen lost her balance while flailing. She fell over the chair's back, landing hard on the bedroom floor. It knocked the wind out of her. Stunned, she lay motionless for a few seconds.

The insects were upon her immediately. She could feel them swarm around her feet and get under her pajama bottoms. The mass scurried up her legs beneath the material. The sensation of a thousand little legs moving across her bare skin mortified her. In an instant, they were at her crotch, pushing, squirming, entering her.

Breath returning to Karen's lungs, she screamed and shook. She fought to sit up. The palmetto bugs coated her face, going for her eyes and mouth. She closed them both again. The persistence of the insects was unbeatable, however, and they forced their way through her tight lips and into her mouth.

Panic set in as Karen was unable to breathe. Gulping for air only allowed more of the bugs into her mouth and throat. Her body convulsed, rapidly weakening, until her eyes fluttered.

Karen's vision faded as she suffocated.

CHAPTER 19
BROTHERLY COUNSEL

The phone rang, waking Lance from his contented sleep. Grumbling, he snapped his eyes open and turned his head toward the nightstand. He reached for his phone and looked to see who was calling. His vision was hazy, having just woken, but he could read Jaelyn's name on the screen. He picked up.

"Hello," he muttered.

"Lance, ohmygod, ohmygod!" Jaelyn's voice was wild with panic. "Oh Lance, Karen's dead!"

Lance's body tightened as a jolt of adrenaline shot through him. "What?" He sat up.

"She's *dead*, Lance! Oh, Jesus, I can't believe it!"

"Are you sure?"

"Yes!" Jaelyn said, hysterical. "Jesus, yes!"

He lifted his feet from the mattress and set them down on the floor. "I'm sorry," he said, realizing the absurdity of his question. "It's just, I can't believe it. Are you okay?"

"No, I'm not okay! Karen's fucking *dead!*"

Another stupid question, he scolded himself. "I'm sorry," he said again. "What happened?"

"I don't know," whimpered Jaelyn. "I just found her in her bedroom this morning, lying on the floor dead. I just got off the phone with the police."

"Jesus. Do you want to come over?"

"Can you come over here?" she pleaded. "I can't leave my sisters."

Lance nodded, though nobody could see it. "Of course." He emerged from his bedroom and walked to the kitchen to start a pot of coffee. "Just sit tight. I'll get David and Jim, and we'll be right over."

"Okay, baby," Jaelyn sobbed. "Thank you."

He hung up. After loading the coffee maker and pressing the button to start brewing, he turned and faced David's bedroom. This news was devastating, and Lance was unsure about how to break it to his roommate. Exhaling laboriously, he walked to David's bedroom and knocked on the closed door.

David's voice growled from the other side. "Whaaaaaat?"

"Dude," said Lance, trying to sound gentle. "You need to get up. Something happened to Karen."

The delayed reaction was expected from somebody that just woke up. "Karen?"

"Yes, Karen. I'm afraid I have some bad news."

"What? Is she okay?"

"Come on out. We need to get over to their house."

A moment passed before David made it to the door

and opened it. "What's going on?" the sleepy Latino queried.

Lance had no idea what the best way to say it was, so he just said it. "Karen's dead. Jaelyn just called and told me."

David's face went white. "What?" Surely his friend was kidding.

"I know. I couldn't believe it either." Lance patted David's arm. "Come on, I've got the coffee started. Get dressed, and we'll head over there."

Then Lance called Jim, waking him up. When he told Jim what had happened, the stunned friend stated he would get up and go to the house with them. By the time Lance and David knocked on his door, he was dressed and ready to join them.

Lance decided to drive the quarter mile between homes. The trio hopped into the Honda, and Lance started driving. As they approached the sorority house, they saw the last of the police vehicles drive away. The sight made David's heart heavy; the truth of Karen's death was now made real to him.

Lance pressed the doorbell. A moment later, Jaelyn opened the door. Her eyes were red from crying. When she saw Lance and the others, the tears flowed once again. "Ohmygod, guys," she blubbered, embracing them all. The group migrated indoors and sat in the living room.

"What happened?" said Lance, his arm around her for comfort.

Jaelyn wiped the tears below her eyes. "I dunno. They said she died of asphyxiation. She just suffocated."

"Suffocated?" David echoed.

"Uh-huh."

Jim scratched his head. "Did she have any food allergies?"

"No, none."

"So, the police deemed it natural causes?" Lance asked.

Jaelyn nodded. "Yeah. They said there was no evidence to suggest otherwise. No signs of an attack, no bruises or cuts, nothing. But Lance, there was nothing 'natural' about her face. Her eyes were still wide open, and her mouth too. Like she tried to scream. She looked terrified." Jaelyn began to sob again. The image of her lifeless friend seared into her brain.

Lance held her tighter. He looked at David while caressing her hair. David's stunned expression captured the helpless feeling shared by all.

The men took Jaelyn away from the gloomy house. They boarded Lance's CR-V and drove to a Waffle House. They wanted to be someplace where they could take a quiet booth and nibble away at some brunch fare.

The group sat, reminisced, laughed, and cried together. They were there for two hours. When they had mourned and eaten enough, the crew left the restaurant and returned to Lance's car. They drove around aimlessly for another hour.

Finally, they decided to hang out at the guys' apartment. They grabbed something to drink from the refrigerator and sat down in the living room. Lance turned on the television for background noise. Instead of watching it, his eyes were idly gazing at the floor.

Jim ran his hands through his long, black hair, pulling it back while he sighed. "I can't believe Karen's gone," he stated. "I would've never guessed anything was wrong with her."

"She was so hung over yesterday," said Jaelyn. "I brought her some food after she woke up, but I didn't see her the rest of the day."

David frowned. "She sounded pretty bad when I called her."

"Yeah. The rest of us went to the movies yesterday without her because she said she just wanted to spend the day in bed. I didn't even bother her last night after we all got back to the house."

"So she never left her room?" asked David.

"Nope," Jaelyn said. "Well, except for when she had to use the bathroom." Then she remembered. "Oh, and she wanted that chest I got from you yesterday. She did say she wanted to do some research on it while she was staying in."

Lance raised his eyebrows slightly but did not alter his blank stare.

David studied Lance for a moment. Lance had the same apathetic expression on his face that David had noticed at the sorority house. A creepy feeling fell over him like Lance was somehow involved in the recent events.

"You know," said David, still looking at Lance, "ever since we found that chest, weird things have been happening. I think it's haunted."

Jaelyn smirked. "What? Come on, David."

"I'm serious! Think about it. It supposedly was buried with a killer named Jack Grainger by a woman who killed him for revenge. We found it in a field occupied by — wait for it — *ghosts*, and look how Todd died! He was skinned, just like 'Jack the Skinner' used to do!"

"Listen to what you're saying," said Lance. "You

sound crazy."

David shook his head. "I'm not crazy, just open-minded. In fact, this is the kind of thing you should tell your ghost-hunting brother about."

Lance leaned forward. "If it's haunted, then maybe we should destroy that chest. Burn it."

"No," David contested. "Not until you talk to your brother. For all we know, we might need it. I'm not taking any chances destroying something we might need later."

"I think that's a good idea," said Jaelyn. "Your brother's a paranormal investigator, right?"

"Right."

"Then you should totally call him and tell him about everything. Just to hear what he thinks about it all."

"You guys are nuts."

David nudged Lance's shoulder. "Come on, man, give him a call. You *did* say something about talking to him when we were in Colorado."

Lance looked at his friends, and he saw that all three of them were waiting for him to comply. "Fine," he finally said. "I'll give him a call." He pulled his phone out, scrolled through his list of contacts, and found his brother's number. He was admittedly nervous about talking to Donnie. They had only spoken a few times since their parents and Donnie had disowned each other. Lance dialed his ousted brother.

After just two rings, Donnie picked up. "Hey, li'l brother!" he said with surprise in his voice.

Hearing Donnie's voice brought a tear to the corner of Lance's eye. He smiled. "Hey, big brother. How are you?"

"I'm good, I'm good. How about you? How's school

going?"

Lance shrugged. "We're in summer break, getting ready for fall classes to start soon."

"I'm glad you called," said Donnie. "I was thinking about you the other night."

"Yeah?"

"Yeah. Had a weird dream. About us being lost in the woods together, trying to find a way out. Silly stuff."

The statement gave Lance a chill, and he leaned back. "I'll tell you what's weird. The reason I'm calling is because we're going through some strange shit here. Supernatural kind of stuff. And we're at a loss about what to do. We thought maybe you could help guide us through it."

"No shit?" Donnie's intrigue was evident. "Tell me."

"Okay. Well, it all started with our trip to Silver Valley."

"Silver Valley?"

"It's a small town in Colorado, in the mountains. Used to be a silver-mining town. Anyway, David and I found something online about ghost lights there."

"Ah," said Donnie. "I'm familiar with those."

"You are?" Then Lance thought about what his brother did for a living. "Of course you are. You're the ghost guy."

"Indeed. Did you get to see any?"

"We did. They were really cool, actually," Lance affirmed. "There's an old graveyard just outside of town. There was a big field past that, where we saw quite a few of them dancing around. Different colors and everything."

"Like the Marfa lights," stated Donnie. "There's a pretty famous phenomenon that occurs here in Texas, and lots of people go there to see it. Scientists too, trying to figure out what's really causing the bright, moving lights at night. But they can't find a scientific explanation for it. I've seen them myself. The Marfa lights are the real deal."

"So are these," said Lance. "They're amazing. I can't even try to describe what they're really like. You have to see them with your own eyes."

"I might just do that someday," Donnie said. "But I have a feeling there's more to your story than that."

Lance cleared his throat. "Yes. There was talk in town about a grave out in the field belonging to a bad character. A killer from the Old West days. And supposedly, his treasure was buried with him in the field."

"Ooh…go on."

"Well, we followed one of the ghost lights—a red one—to a specific area where the grave was." Lance closed his eyes. "And we uncovered a small, wooden chest there."

"And?"

"And there was nothing in it. Well, except that one time."

"Yes?"

Lance hesitated before continuing. "Cockroaches came out when we first opened it. Palmetto bugs, actually. Like, a *ton* of them. More than could've fit in there. And then when we opened it and looked inside again, they were completely gone. It was like they never existed."

"What?" Donnie sounded concerned. "That sounds like some kind of spirit manifestation. That's not good."

"Apparently not," said Lance. "Because a lot of bad stuff has happened to us since then. The guy who rented us our motel room was found killed there, right after we left."

"Jesus!"

"And two people have died mysteriously here at school in the last week. One of them was with us in Colorado."

"Wait a minute," said Donnie. "You said the light you followed in the field was red?"

"Bright red," Lance confirmed. "Why do you ask?"

"Well," Donnie informed, "when it comes to ghost lights, their color usually indicates what type of spirit they are. Red can mean anger and obsession."

"Great."

"Do you still have that chest?" Donnie asked.

"Not with us," said Lance, looking over at his roommate. "But the chest is someplace safe."

"Good," Donnie said. "Keep it secure somewhere. And whatever you do, don't open it again."

Lance nodded. "Okay, we won't."

"Listen, I've got something I need to wrap up here. But how about I drive up there and see you in a few days when I'm done?"

Lance wanted that. "Sounds good, Donnie."

"All right, little brother. Let me write down your address there."

Lance gave Donnie his address, talked for a few more minutes, and then said goodbye. Speaking with his big brother left him with a warm feeling. It made him realize it had been too long since their last conversation. Much too long.

CHAPTER 20
SEEKING HELP

Jim was somewhere in the desert. Sheltered from the sun beneath a sandstone cliff, he was able to look out across the plain before him. All he saw was sand, yucca, and tumbleweed. A hollow-sounding wind traveled by, deep and ominous. It almost sounded like a warning.

Some movement caught Jim's eye, and he turned his head. The motion came from a cluster of cacti near him. There, amid the saguaros and prickly pears, something was stirring the sand from beneath. Jim stepped closer to investigate.

A hand breached the surface of the sand. Then it rose as if being pulled by an invisible rope, bringing its arm with it. A black cowboy hat emerged from the desert next. Under that was the shaded head of a man.

Jim was in awe of the rising man. The stranger's body was seemingly being born from the sand. Defying gravity, it effortlessly slid upward from the ground until the man was standing on the desert surface. Around six feet tall and covered with sand granules, the stranger in the cowboy hat brushed away some of the grit and dust. Then he lifted his head and looked at Jim.

It was Lance.

Frowning with confusion, Jim took a step backward. What was Lance doing in the desert? And more importantly, how did he ascend after being buried in the sand? As if hearing the questions in Jim's mind, Lance reared his head back and smiled.

Jim sensed something unusual about Lance's face. He looked closer. Then he saw it; Lance's eyes were different. One was significantly darker than normal, and the other was not visible at all.

It was like he was *wearing* someone else's eyes.

Or somebody else was wearing Lance.

Lance's arm suddenly raised, a finger pointed at Jim. Then a laugh spilled out from Lance's mouth. Jim knew immediately that it was not Lance's voice.

Jim woke. His eyes popped open, and he gazed around his bedroom. Seeing the comfort of daylight filtering through the blinds, he relaxed. The night was over.

It had been a rough night. The teeth had visited him once again, and once again, he had to fight off the visions with his mind. His meditation eventually sent the ghostly teeth away. But the addition of the disturbing dream ensured that Jim did not get a good night's sleep.

He got up and shuffled toward the kitchen. He yearned for a hot cup of coffee. Jim started a pot, then moved to the living area to turn on the TV. He searched for something to watch while he waited for his coffee to brew.

As he sat on the couch, he reflected on his dream. Why did Lance appear to him as someone else? Sure, Lance had been behaving differently lately. There were little things like he no longer replied with the word *"kanpai"* when Jim gave his *"banzai"* toast. No big deal. But Lance no longer seemed to have his irritable bowel syndrome, which was nothing short of a scientific miracle. And the fact that he practically owned the frat guy that one afternoon was unexplainable.

Okay, Lance had changed significantly.

And it all seemed to start during their trip to the mountains chasing ghosts. Ever since they had opened that chest they found buried in the field. Jim contemplated the mysterious army of palmetto bugs, the spectral visions haunting Jim at night, the unusual deaths of Todd and Karen, and the undeniable fact that Lance was no longer the same person.

After connecting all the dots, Jim came to the conclusion that something was terribly wrong with his neighbor: he was likely possessed.

So, what now? Jim pondered. The first thing that came to mind was an exorcism. He quickly discounted that thought, however. That was something that only happened in movies. But then he realized those movies were inspired by true cases of something evil being expelled from afflicted people.

Hell, his own ancestors had such ceremonies. After letting that soak in, Jim reconsidered the idea of an exorcism. But not a Christian one.

He would contact the Zuni tribe for help.

Jim recalled the members of the tribe that he knew. The best candidate was obviously Martin Dewa. Martin was a tribal medicine man, a shaman, and also a friend of Jim's family. And Martin Dewa lived not two hours away.

Jim called his parents to get the number for Martin. After chatting with his folks for twenty minutes, Jim got the phone number from his father. He finished talking with his parents and dialed the medicine man.

***

Martin's phone rang four times, and then he picked up. "Hello?"

"Hello, Mr. Dewa. This is Jim Laverdure. You know, Walter's son."

"Yes," Martin responded. "I know you, Jim. How are you? Are you still in school?"

"I'm good, still plugging away here at ASU."

"Good to hear. Education is something that can never be taken away from you."

"Speaking of education, sort of, let me tell you why I called," said Jim. "I need some of your guidance."

Martin was curious since he was the one being called instead of Jim's father. "What would you like to know?"

"Well," Jim began, "I have a friend here at school who I think is maybe, um, possessed."

"Possessed, you say!"

"Yes, sir. See, we all went to look for ghosts in the mountains, found a buried chest that is supposed to belong to an evil man, and we brought it back with us."

Martin felt his skin tingle.

"Ever since," continued Jim, "bad things have been happening near us. A student was killed, one of our friends died mysteriously in her room, and I've been having visions at night."

"What kinds of visions?"

"Unexplainable stuff — teeth that materialize in midair and come after me."

"I see. You are dealing with a bad spirit, young man."

"I've been able to send the visions away each night with meditation," said Jim, "But it is difficult. They keep coming back. And I see changes in my friend Lance. He is not himself; I believe he has been affected by the presence of the ghost, or spirit, or what-have-you, of the evil man associated with the old chest. I feel that if we can expel the entity from Lance, then all of the visions will go away as well.

"So," Jim concluded, "I have to ask you for help. We need you to hold a ritual and use your power to get rid of the spirit that's tormenting us."

Martin cleared his throat. "I cannot perform this ceremony on a white man," he stated apologetically.

"Then will you tell me how, and I will do it?"

"No, you are not a shaman."

Jim understood the traditional exclusivity of the Zuni rituals, but he was not willing to accept it. His friend needed help, regardless of his heritage. "Look, he's my friend. I have to try. If you don't help me, I'll find another who will."

Martin contemplated for a long moment. If Jim went to somebody else who was unqualified to deal with the bad spirit, he could receive the wrong information and end up making things worse. "All right," he agreed. "But this is against my wishes. I cannot teach you the ceremonies I know unless you are to become a shaman. But come over, and I will show you some things that will help you drive the spirit away."

There was a great relief in Jim's voice. "Thank you, Mr. Dewa. I'll drive up to see you today. You're a lifesaver."

CHAPTER 21
THE RITUAL

It rained heavily the following morning. A summer monsoon was coming through, drenching the desert city.

"It's a good thing classes didn't start this week," David remarked, gazing out the living room window. "That's shitty weather to be out walking in."

"Yep," said Lance, sipping his coffee. He was focused on the television. "It's a good day for staying in and being lazy."

David heard a ping from his phone, notifying him of new activity. He went to the phone and checked the display. Jim had just sent him a text message. It told David to come next door to Jim's place.

Shrugging, David grabbed his coffee cup and headed for the door. "Jim needs something," he said to Lance, who was captivated by the television program. "I'll be back."

"Okay."

David left the apartment and went to Jim's, keeping

close to the wall to utilize as much of the awning as he could to keep from getting wet. He knocked on the door, and Jim promptly let him in.

"What's up?" David said, wiping his wet shoes on the doorway mat.

"Come on in," Jim welcomed. "I've got to talk to you about something."

"Okay." David followed Jim into the living area and sat on the couch. Taking a sip of his coffee, he noticed an abundance of strange items decorating the room. "When did you get all this stuff?"

"Yesterday," said Jim. "I visited a medicine man from my tribe."

David raised an eyebrow. That was an unusual way to spend a Monday. "Okay then. We were wondering where you were yesterday."

"All right," Jim started. "What I'm going to tell you is a little out there. But you have to promise me you'll hear me out."

David grinned, interested. "Okay. What's on your mind?"

"Like I said, I visited a medicine man. I needed to find someone who can help us."

"With?"

"Well, I told you about the visions I've been having, the damn teeth."

"Yeah. And I told you to lay off the drugs."

Jim sat straighter, looking cross. "You said you'd listen."

David's grin dissolved; he could tell that what was on

Jim's mind was serious. "Okay, sorry. You're right."

"Ever since we got back from Colorado, we've had some strange shit happen. My visions that keep attacking me, what happened to the frat boy, poor Karen, and especially Lance. He doesn't act or talk like he used to. He doesn't even get the shits anymore."

"Come to think of it," said David. "The other day, he swore to me that he'd seen an *eyeball* in his bedroom. And he *has* been acting differently since we got back."

"He visited me in a dream the other night," Jim added. "His body raised itself right out of the ground and faced me. But the eyes weren't his, and neither was the voice. So, after all that, I've figured it out. A bad spirit has attached itself to Lance. Something that came back with us from that field in Colorado. And we need to get rid of it."

David was stunned to hear what Jim was telling him, but at the same time, it did not completely surprise him. Something deep inside David must have felt the same way. "So, *how* do we get rid of it?" David finally asked.

"I have everything I need for a ceremony. We just need to convince Lance to come over and let me perform it on him."

"Not anything painful or weird, is it?"

"No," Jim chuckled. "I'm not going to string him up or anything like that. He just needs to lie on the couch and let me draw the spirit out of him."

"Hmm," said David. "Worth a shot." He stood up. "C'mon, let's go talk to him and see what he says."

David brought Jim back to his apartment. When they entered, Lance turned his head to see them come in.

Jim nodded to Lance. "Hey, dude."

Lance gave a head bob. "Hey, Jim. What's going on with you?"

Jim and David looked at each other, then at Lance. "Well," said Jim, "I have an experiment I need your help with."

"Oh?"

"Yeah. It's kind of a spiritual thing I think I need to do."

Lance smirked. "Like what? Running around campus naked?"

"No," said David, adding his support. "This has more to do with ghosts. Probably one in particular."

The slender student seemed intrigued. "Really? Like a séance? Summoning a spirit from the afterlife?"

Jim tilted his head. "More like sending one back *to* the afterlife."

Lance wrinkled his brow. "You mean like an exorcism?"

"It's a Zuni ceremony," Jim clarified. "For expelling unwelcome spirits."

"Okay...and just what do you need *my* help with?"

Jim cleared his throat. "I need you to be the subject. Actually, it's more like *I'm* gonna help *you*."

Lance's body tightened defensively. "You can't be serious."

"I think you should do it," said David. "It'll be good for you."

"You're crazy," Lance sighed.

"Come on," David urged, "all it could do is help."

"Dude, what is the point? You think something's *wrong* with me? Something that a crazy *Indian ritual* will fix?"

"I do," Jim stated. "Whether you know it or not. You have to trust me, Bowser. I see that you are not yourself."

Lance chuckled. "Well, if I start puking green pea soup, or if my head spins all the way around, then we'll talk about this."

"I'm not saying there's a *demon* in you," Jim explained, "but there is definitely a spirit that has attached itself to you."

"I'm not possessed," scoffed Lance.

"Then you won't mind humoring us," said Jim.

"You're silly." Lance looked at David, who stood next to Jim with his arms folded. Both friends looked back at Lance earnestly as if they would not take no for an answer.

Go ahead, he heard his thoughts declare. *That heathen ritual can't do anything to you.*

"You know what? Fine," said Lance. He got to his feet. "Let's do this silly thing and get it over with."

The sky of the late morning had grown a little darker. The clouds had thickened, and a burst of rain was pouring down. The group hurried along the balcony to Jim's apartment.

As soon as they stepped inside, Lance felt uncomfortable. He was not sure why—he had been here before, many times—but for some reason, it felt wrong today. His eyes scanned the apartment and quickly found the items Jim had obtained yesterday.

There was a medicine bag on the coffee table, made from buckskin and accented with fringes. Next to it sat a pot molded from red clay. Two sticks were there, each about a foot long, as was a long strand of yucca with one end frayed open. At the end of the table were several dolls and figurines.

Three kachina dolls were placed standing upright. The

warriors were carved from cottonwood root and painted, and one of them was dressed in fabric and adorned with feathers. Smaller figures, called fetishes, stood around the kachina warriors. Some were wood carvings of animals, the largest being a black bear, the most powerful of the beast gods. The other wemawes, as Martin had called them, were sculpted from stone to represent the spirits of deities and animals with healing powers, including an eagle and two more bears.

See? Lance asserted. *Heathen silliness.* He and David followed Jim into the living room.

Jim held his hands up. "Now, before we get started, I have to give you fair warning. Some of the things I'm gonna do are things you might not like. But you must stay still for this to work."

Lance merely smirked. "I can take what you've got."

The others could not quite tell if Lance was trying to be funny or foreboding.

"All right then," said Jim. "Come on over here." He gestured to the couch, and Lance walked to it and sat. "Lie down," Jim directed. "And remember — stay still."

Lance lay on the couch and stared at the ceiling. "This is so dumb," he grumbled.

"You said a medicine man showed you how to do this ritual?" David asked.

"Yep," nodded Jim. "And I'm actually gonna do a *series* of rituals. Cleansing, healing, and soul strengthening. Have a seat in the chair there; I'm gonna get started."

"You got it." David was fascinated to see this. He sat in Jim's recliner and watched.

Jim lifted the lid from a clay pot on his coffee table in

the middle of the room. Inside was some incense the shaman had given him to burn. It was a mix of datura, tenatsali, and a few sacred ingredients. Jim lit the incense. A bitter smell permeated the room, turning sweet after a few seconds.

Next, Jim picked up one of the sticks and placed it next to the pot. He produced a bag of corn meal from his pocket and sprinkled some near the prayer stick. This was the offering to bridge the natural and spiritual worlds.

The three young men were starting to feel woozy. Whatever the concoction of incense was, it was loosening their minds. Their mental barriers softened. They were ready for whatever journey was ahead.

Jim began performing a kachina dance, accompanied by a song chant read from a piece of notebook paper. David leaned back in his chair. He was shocked at the volume of Jim's voice. And he had never heard the Zuni language spoken. It captivated him.

Lance, on the other hand, broke out laughing. Jim's initial reaction was to be upset; his friend was cruelly mocking him for trying to help. But then Jim realized another possibility. It was likely that the entity inside Lance was attempting to distract Jim, to throw him off, to prevent him from properly carrying out the ceremony.

Jim smiled, unaffected, and continued. *If I can ward off the evil visions in my bedroom each night,* he encouraged himself, *I can surely be the shaman to send Lance's bad spirit away.*

The young Zuni then picked up the second stick and the yucca strand. He placed the yamuwe stick on the floor next to the couch. Standing over Lance, Jim began reading passages from the paper, also in the native language.

As Jim repeated a phrase, he suddenly came down
with the yucca strand and whipped Lance across the chest. It
was not painful, but it did take Lance by surprise. He quickly
collected himself.

"Oh Jim," he taunted playfully, "whip me."

David smiled, wanting to join in the joking, but he kept
his comments to himself. He would not add to the interruption.

Unfazed, Jim continued repeating the phrase. His voice
rose in volume as his incantation grew more passionate. He
persisted with the ceremonial whipping as well.

Lance had a wry smile on his face. It was impish, almost
daunting. But soon, Lance began to feel nervous, troubled.
His smile diminished. Then he was taken by the sensation of
panic. His stomach muscles began to cramp.

Jim noticed that Lance was no longer smiling. In fact,
he looked angry. Jim had to keep going. He moved forward
with the text, reciting a new passage. He then ended the
phrase by spitting on Lance.

At once, the room felt colder.

Jim sensed a new presence in the room with them. He
froze for a moment, not sure what to do next.

A loud cracking noise was heard, causing Jim and
David to jump. The wooden bear had split in half. They
watched as it then splintered and fell apart on the table.

Suddenly the stone wemawes flew across the room as
if hurled angrily. Jim and David ducked, covering their faces
with their arms. The small carvings bounced against the walls
of the apartment and clacked lifelessly to the floor.

A flash of lightning was visible through the curtains.
Its thunderclap resounded immediately, shaking the walls of

the apartment. The lights went out as the power died.

CHAPTER 22
RETRIBUTION

"Fuck this!" said David, springing to his feet. "That's enough!"

Jim had already arrived at the same conclusion. He moved to the window and opened the curtains to let more light in. "Holy shit," he stammered. He and David looked at Lance on the couch.

He appeared dazed like he had just woken. He raised himself to a sitting position and grimaced. "I don't feel so hot," he said. One of his hands went to his stomach. Then he got up and rushed to the bathroom to throw up.

"Dude," said David, his eyes meeting Jim's. "Did we really just see all that shit?"

Jim was still trying to calm his heart rate. "I'm afraid so, amigo. We just saw some supernatural activity."

David glanced at the remains of the black bear figure. "How do you suppose something like *that* could happen? The wood just split and fell apart."

Jim shrugged. "Your guess is as good as mine." He went to the coffee table to study the damage. The bear was destroyed, but he would return the remains to the shaman anyway. He then looked on the floor to see the kachina warriors. Something was wrong with them too. Upon closer inspection, Jim noticed the heads of the dolls had been wrenched around to face backward.

"Shit," he muttered.

David saw the same thing, and a shiver raced down his spine. "Dude, that's messed up." He held his hands up in front of him. "I think this whole thing was a bad idea, Jim." He sounded scared.

"It did something," Jim stated. "I think I drew something out of him. And it got mad, had a tantrum."

David wandered around the room and picked up the rock wemawes that had been scattered. "That's an understatement," said David. He brought the figures he had gathered to the coffee table and piled them in the middle by the smoking pot. "Should we put that out?" he suggested, the fumes starting to get to him.

"Huh-uh," said Jim. "I wanna let it burn. It needs to finish cleansing the room."

Lance emerged from the bathroom. He did not seem well at all.

"You okay, man?" asked his roommate.

Lance shook his head slowly. "No, I'm not. I think it's that shit," he said, pointing to the burning incense. "Making me sick. I gotta get out of here. I'm going back to our place."

"All right, Bowser," said Jim. "I hope you feel better."

He nodded. "Thanks. I'll catch you later." He trudged

toward the door, and David went with him.

The roommates returned to their own apartment, and Lance headed directly for the couch. Looking like he was still woozy, he plopped onto the cushion and sighed wearily. David got him a glass of water and brought it to the living room. He handed it to Lance.

"Thanks," Lance said. He slowly drank until the glass was empty. "Oh, man, I needed that."

"Feeling any better?" asked David, concerned about his best friend's condition.

"A little. My stomach is queasy. That damn hippie incense of Jim's, I'm sure."

"Sorry, dude. We just thought it would help you."

"You guys are crazy," Lance whispered, blankly looking up. He reflected on the experience of the ritual, and his stomach began to cramp again. "I need to go lie down." Lance took his time walking to his bedroom. He shut the door behind him.

David wondered if Lance would be okay. There was nothing more he could do for his friend now, however, except let him rest. Besides, David was dying to talk with Jim about the morning's activity. He locked up the apartment and went over to Jim's.

"How's he doing?' Jim asked when David entered.

"Stomach's bothering him," replied David. "He went to bed. He looked exhausted."

Jim believed it. "Been through a lot. That is if the ceremony went the way I think it did."

"And if it didn't?"

"You mean what if it didn't work?"

David nodded.

"I dunno, then I guess we just look for another way. But don't worry; I'm sure the ceremony worked."

David and Jim hung out for a while, discussing how Jim was able to get the ritual items and how he was going to have to explain what happened to them when he returned them to their owner. Surely the shaman would understand. He knew what they were going to be used for and would not hold it against Jim if the angry spirit damaged the items.

The duo eventually decided to walk somewhere for lunch. The rain had stopped, so they had no need for an umbrella on their journey. The hungry students were soon inside a restaurant and enjoying some hearty food. Eventually, David decided he needed to get back and check on Lance. The two made their way back to the apartment complex.

When Jim returned to his place, he thought about what David had feared. What if the ritual didn't work? What else could be done to help Lance if there was still a spirit inside him?

Jim went to his bedroom and turned on his computer. After it fired up and found an Internet connection, Jim began searching the web for effective ways of expelling spirits. He found quite a lot.

Scrolling down the list of results, he saw an abundance of suggestions. There was simple prayer. There were universal all-calls, where the person calls out to the universe, instead of a deity, for help. There was the use of white light. There was smudging, which was the process of cleansing by burning sage.

Jim felt something bite his shoulder.

"Ow," he said out loud. Frowning, he looked at his shoulder. Nothing was there. He slapped his hand roughly onto the spot, just in case there was a spider inside his shirt, and rubbed the area forcefully.

Jim resumed his search for spirit expulsions. He came across an article about orgonite, a molded epoxy compound containing quartz crystals. Small metal chips, like aluminum, copper, and iron pyrite, were included during production to help draw in orgone energy waves, absorb them, and transform them. Sometimes labeled as a "holy hand grenade," its placement in a room with a negative spirit was said to convert that energy and direct it to move on.

He felt another bite, this time on his stomach. Quickly raising his shirt to investigate, Jim once again saw nothing. A third bite occurred. This one was more painful. He looked closer and could see a small spot of redness instantly appear, but he could not see what was attacking him. He felt the skin begin to itch where he had been bitten.

"What the fuck!" he exclaimed.

Suddenly he felt bites all over his midsection, like little, excruciating pinches, occurring simultaneously, relentlessly, repeatedly.

"*Jesus!*" he squealed. Although Jim could not see anything on his skin, something was definitely attacking him. Red spots surfaced like a downpour of raindrops on a sidewalk. He feverishly brushed and scratched at his body in an attempt to repel the unseen assailants. He thought of fleas, bedbugs, or other minuscule parasites, with their tiny mouths, sharp teeth, and ravenous appetites for blood. The thought only made him panic and scratch harder, more voraciously.

Everything itched. No matter how hard Jim scratched, it became worse. It was maddening. Jim lurched out of his chair, stumbled, and landed on the floor next to his bed. He could feel each tiny bite of the frenzy, little teeth everywhere. The itching was unbearable. Jim cried out, digging harder against his skin with his fingernails. His skin quickly gave way, and blood began to surface where he tore the tissue.

Jim knew he was bleeding, but he was too crazed to care. He had to do something about the ceaseless itching. Screaming, he scratched incessantly, violently, with the same fervor as a frustrated rabbit or cat with annoying fleas, digging even deeper into the tracks his nails had just created. Within moments his body was raw and coated in blood.

There was a knock on the door, but Jim could not hear it over his own cries. Another knock, and then the door opened. David, having heard the screaming from next door, stood at the doorway.

"Jim?" he said, entering the apartment. "You okay?" The cries drew him to Jim's bedroom. There David's eyes took in the sight of the bloody, mutilated young man. "Jesus!" David yelped. He rushed to the shaking, gruesome mass on the floor. "What the fuck happened?"

Jim could not answer. Instead, he continued to scrape away his itching skin. David hurriedly pulled out his phone and called 911. After telling the dispatcher the nature of the emergency and his location, he sat down on the floor next to Jim.

"What the fuck, Jim?" David burbled, tears rolling down his face.

Jim had little life left in him. Too weak to speak, he

mustered whatever strength he had left to keep scratching. David wrapped his arms around Jim's, grabbing them at the wrists and holding them still.

David could feel the blood soak through his shirt and stick to his own skin. "Help is coming, Jim," he promised with a quivering voice. "Just hang on. I've got you."

David held his weakened friend tightly, refusing to let Jim slip away.

CHAPTER 23
THE ASSESSMENT

"Lance, get up."

He heard the voice on the other side of the bedroom door, accompanied by knocking. Looking at the clock, Lance realized he had been sleeping for hours. He was groggy. But at least he no longer felt ill.

"Lance!"

"What?" he moaned.

David opened the door. "Dude, we've gotta go. They just took Jim to the hospital."

Lance's eyes focused, and he saw Jim's blood covering David. The sight jolted him awake. "Holy shit! What happened?"

David buried his face in his hands. "I don't know, man. I heard him screaming, went over there, and found him...." He did not know how to finish the sentence.

"Found him what?"

"Jesus...he had ripped most of his skin off."

"*What?*"

"Come on, let's go. We should be at the hospital with him."

The shock of the dire news motivated Lance. "Yeah, give me a second." He nodded at the bloody clothes clinging to David. "You might want to change first."

The paramedics had told David they were taking Jim to Tempe St. Luke's after they wrapped him up and laid him in the back of the ambulance. The hospital was conveniently close to campus. David and Lance walked the four blocks to St. Luke's.

They went into the emergency room entrance and approached the desk. David stated who they were there to see, and the receptionist told them to have a seat in the waiting room. Minutes later, a nurse came over to speak with them.

"He's in surgery right now," she informed them.

"Is he gonna be okay?" asked David.

"Someone will come down and talk to you about it later, once they've stabilized him. Do you know if he has any allergies?"

"I don't think so, but I don't know," Lance admitted. "He doesn't live with us; he's our neighbor."

"Okay. Just sit tight. In the meantime, if you need anything, let one of us know."

The men thanked the nurse and watched her disappear behind the swinging doors. With a deep exhale, they settled into their chairs and began what was sure to be a long wait.

Several hours later, a doctor emerged from within and found the students. The middle-aged woman sat down to speak with them.

"How's Jim doing?" asked David.

"He's in the ICU," the doctor stated. "He's stable now, but we'll just have to wait and see. It's a miracle he survived that much blood loss. We had to do a lot of skin grafting."

David could still feel the sensation of Jim's blood matting his shirt against his skin. He shuddered. "That was a lot of blood."

"Did he take any drugs?"

"No," said David. "We lit some incense earlier, which made us a little woozy, but that was all. And not to get high," he clarified. "It was part of an Indian ritual Jim was doing with us."

"Do you know what was in that incense?"

"Not really. Some different flowers and stuff. Whatever the medicine man gave to Jim."

"It's possible the incense caused a hallucinatory reaction. He said something about bugs biting him all over. Did either of the two of you see or feel unusual after being near the incense?"

The pair shook their heads.

"Interesting," the doctor said. "It must be that Jim has some type of allergy to what was in the incense, and you two do not."

"Possible," said Lance, but he was not so sure.

"What if he wasn't hallucinating?" David feared.

"There was no evidence of any bites that we could see. No, I think he had a reaction to something that made him hallucinate. Drove him crazy."

"Crazy enough to scratch his skin off?" said David, skeptical.

"I've seen it before," the doctor informed. "It happens more than you would think with substances like methamphetamine and LSD."

"When can we see him?" asked Lance.

"Go home, get some sleep, and come back tomorrow to check his condition. We'll see how he's doing then, okay?"

After the long hours of worrying in the waiting room, the roommates reluctantly agreed; they needed to eat something and then go home for the night. The doctor offered a reassuring smile and walked away.

"I'm starving," said David, realizing the sun had already gone down. "I think we need to get some dinner on the way back."

Lance nodded slightly, gazing directly ahead. He caught sight of his own reflection in one of the dark windows. Something about the dull image disturbed him.

His faint reflection was smiling furtively, victoriously, back at him.

PART III

CHAPTER 24
THE VISITOR

Lance was on the couch facing the television. Not actually watching the midday talk show, he was staring through the TV. His mind was focused on something else completely.

There was a knock at the door. Lance snapped to and looked at David, seated next to him. David simply shrugged and returned his attention to his phone. Realizing he was going to have to address the visitor, Lance got to his feet and shambled to the door.

To his surprise, his brother Donnie was standing outside. The older sibling smiled, and his eyes glistened a bit at the sight of Lance.

"What's up, li'l bro?" he beamed, stretching his arms wide.

Lance hesitated for the briefest moment. Something inside him was trying to restrain his bursting emotions. But the uncontrollable urge to embrace his brother won out. He gave Donnie a strong hug.

"My God, Donnie," said Lance, his eyes also dampening. "How long has it been?"

Donnie had to think about it. It had been almost two years since his falling out with his parents. He had spoken with Lance on the phone now and then but had not physically seen him since Donnie was disowned. "Way too long," he replied.

"Hell, man, come on in."

Donnie followed his brother inside. "Not a bad place," he said, noting the spacious layout of the apartment. Then he saw David looking at him from the couch.

"You remember David, don't you?" said Lance.

"Of course I do," smiled Donnie. "Long time no see, David."

David stood and walked over to meet their guest. "How's it going, Donnie? Good to see you again."

"You too, man."

"Oh, hey," thought Lance, "want some coffee?"

"Heck yeah," said Donnie enthusiastically. "I've been on the road since early this morning."

"Where'd you come from?" asked David.

"I stayed the night in Las Cruces, left around five to have less traffic."

"You're still living in Texas, right?" Lance said.

Donnie nodded. "Yep. Just outside San Antonio. Drove nine hours from there yesterday, and then another six hours from Las Cruces today."

Lance handed his brother a cup of coffee. "Well, it's good to see you. I've missed you."

Donnie gave his brother another hug. "Missed you too, li'l bro."

Lance caught himself studying his brother. He looked exactly as he had years ago. The same crooked smile, the same dimples, and his light-brown hair was even styled as it always had been, parted in the middle and feathered back on the sides.

"You haven't changed one bit," Lance remarked. "You look just like you did back in high school."

"You've changed a little," said Donnie. "You don't look as much like a little kid as you used to."

David chuckled. "He's changed, all right. Although he won't admit it."

Donnie furrowed his brow. "What do you mean?"

"David…," sighed Lance.

The Latino ignored his roommate. "We think he was possessed."

Donnie recoiled. "What?"

"By the ghost of some murderous cowboy, 'Black Jack' Grainger. The one we think that chest Lance told you about belongs to. Jim, our next-door neighbor, did an Indian exorcism ritual on Lance a couple of days ago. Some weird stuff happened, like statues being thrown across the room."

Donnie eyed his brother with concern. "Lance, that's serious shit. How do you feel?"

Lance rolled his eyes. "I'm fine. I think they were just high from whatever was in that incense Jim was burning."

"Yeah, whatever," scoffed David. "I wasn't high when I found Jim bleeding to death."

"Whoa," said Donnie. "What the hell?"

"I heard him screaming next door, went inside, and saw him just scratching himself like a mad man. He said something about being bitten by bugs, couldn't get them off him, and he had literally scraped most of his skin away. He almost died from the blood loss."

"Jesus." Donnie stared at the floor, processing what he had just heard. He shuddered at the image his mind produced.

"Let's go sit down," suggested Lance. The trio sat on the couch to continue their conversation.

"Comfy couch," said Donnie. It felt good compared to the seat in his van.

"You can crash here if you like," Lance offered. "It's no trouble."

"Naw, I already booked a motel room nearby. It's the Motel 6 back there on Apache Boulevard."

Lance nodded. "Sure, I know where that is."

"So, what's been going on with you?" asked Donnie. "I mean, besides the stuff you called me about. School going okay?"

"Yeah, not too bad."

"Got a girlfriend?"

Lance sat up straight and proud. "I do. Her name's Jaelyn, and she's amazing."

Donnie was taken aback. "Really? That's awesome. Good for you."

"Yeah," said David. "She's a sorority girl, but she's actually really cool. And she and Lance are good together."

"That's great," said Donnie, happy to hear his little brother had found companionship.

"How 'bout you?" Lance queried. "Any special girl in

your life right now?"

"Naw, not at the moment," admitted Donnie. "But I've been so busy working I don't think too much about having time for girls."

"How's the ghost hunting business?" asked David. "I'm dying to hear about some of the stuff you do."

"It's okay," Donnie said with a grin. "Not everybody's cup of tea, but I love it. And I've seen *soooo* much cool shit."

David leaned forward eagerly. "Yeah? Like what?"

"Oh, man," smiled Donnie, leaning back. "I've heard knocking in an empty room, ghosts' voices that I've recorded, seen poltergeist activity, misty figures moving around in abandoned asylums, and ghost lights in Marfa."

"You should check out the ghost lights up in Colorado!" said David excitedly. "They were so cool to see. Different colors, sizes, speeds, just dancing around in the field."

Donnie nodded. "Yep, Lance told me about that. Sounds like a place I should definitely go see."

"It's cool," Lance confirmed.

Donnie shifted on his cushion. "I want to see that old chest you told me about," he said. There was urgency in his tone. "I'm really curious to get a look at that and check it out."

"You think us bringing it down here was a bad idea?" David said, already believing it was.

"Probably. Especially if it's associated with the ghost of someone who was evil."

"Oh, the dude was evil, all right," stated David. "This guy Jack Grainger allegedly killed tons of Indians, prospectors, and whoever else was in his way."

"Jack Grainger?" Donnie repeated, making a mental

note. "You mentioned him earlier."

"Yeah," said David. "He also has nicknames like 'Black Jack' and 'Jack the Skinner.'"

Donnie felt a chill. "Okay, I can guess how he got the 'skinner' nickname. I'll have to dig up some stuff about him online."

"Do you think he could be haunting us?" asked David.

"Entirely possible," said Donnie. "Many times, a spirit is attached to an earthly object. Sometimes for fondness, sometimes because it can't get away."

"There *was* the Louisiana woman."

"What?"

"Yeah," David elaborated, "a woman from Louisiana that came up to Colorado after she found out about her brother being murdered by Jack Grainger. She supposedly killed Grainger and buried some of his remains in the chest."

"Louisiana...wow, that might explain the palmetto bugs. They're all over in the South, where this woman came from." Donnie grew excited. "Okay, I've got to see this damn chest."

"It's over at...Karen's," Lance said gently. "At the sorority house. We can go over there later."

"You should check out Jim's place," offered David. "It's right next door, and we had some scary shit happen over there the day Jim ended up trying to scratch himself to death."

"I'm game," Donnie grinned. "Can we get in?"

"Yeah," said Lance. "We all have a copy of each others' keys since we're always hanging out together."

"Come on," said Donnie, returning to his feet. "Let's go check it out."

"What, right now?" said Lance.

"Sure, why not? The sooner I get started, the better."

David pulled Jim's spare key from the wall hook. The trio then migrated next door to unlock Jim's apartment. David opened the door, and the three went inside.

Donnie sniffed the air. "I smell ozone," he stated.

"Probably that nasty incense Jim was burning," said Lance.

"No, this is different. I smell the medicine flower, but there's also ozone. It's distinct. And it lingers in a place where spirit activity occurs. It indicates ectoplasm. Something supernatural definitely happened here."

David looked smugly at Lance. "See? We weren't high, dude. You were possessed. And the figures Jim had for the ritual got thrown all over the room."

"Physical manifestation," Donnie nodded. "We'd better get the gear out of my van. I want to take some readings and recordings here." He patted his sibling on the shoulder. "Come on, you can give me a hand."

The group strolled down the stairs and through the parking lot. Donnie's vehicle was an old Dodge Ram conversion van. It had a plain, brown exterior that appeared rather dull. Lance was surprised Donnie had not put his business logo on the side of the van.

Going in through the side door, they saw a roomy interior. Donnie had installed steel cabinets against the driver-side wall. A mini-refrigerator was built in next to the side door. In the rear was a small, square table surrounded on three sides by cushioned seats.

"I like your office," David commented.

"Thanks," said Donnie. "That tabletop actually comes down to turn that whole section into a bed. Just have to put the two extra cushions on top of it."

"That's cool," Lance grinned. "You could sleep in here."

"I have," admitted Donnie. "It's not very comfortable, though." He turned his attention to one of the cabinets, twisting the key that unlocked it. He pulled out a canvas bag and several pieces of equipment. "Here you go," he said, handing some to Lance. "All right, let's get back up there." He locked the van up, and the group returned to Jim's apartment.

The first thing Donnie did was turn his EMF meter on. The size of a TV remote control, it measured electromagnetic frequencies. Within seconds its LED array turned from green to red.

"Some strong reading," said Donnie. He surveyed the room. "Otherwise, calm." He reached into the bag and produced a thermal camera. Panning it around, he noted that no thermal images appeared on the screen. He frowned.

"Let's try something else," Donnie said, turning to his brother. "Here, gimme that." Lance handed over the piece Donnie was pointing to—a digital recorder. "I use this to capture EVP—electronic voice phenomena. I'll ask questions, and later we'll see if there are any ghost voices on the playback."

Donnie pressed the record button and began speaking. "If there is a presence in this room, let yourself be known." He paused. "Who is here with us?" Another pause. "Please speak to us; let us know you are here." Another pause. "I want you to show us a sign that you are here."

After a minute of silence, Donnie stopped the recorder and set it down. He brought a camcorder and collapsed tripod out of the canvas bag. He attached the camcorder to the top of the tripod and extended the legs.

"Now we're getting serious," said David.

Donnie smirked. "Yep, time for the heavy artillery. This is a full-spectrum camcorder with night vision. I'll set it up and leave it here, then we'll see if it records anything."

Gathering everything but the camera, the crew left Jim's apartment and went back to their own. There they drank coffee and continued to catch up.

Jaelyn called a short time later. Lance answered the phone and told her she should come over to meet his brother. She was excited to do so. She arrived at the apartment half an hour later.

"You must be Donnie," she said upon seeing the new face. She extended her right hand. "Hi, I'm Jaelyn."

Donnie took her hand with both of his. "Very nice to meet you, Jaelyn."

She kissed Lance, then looked back at Donnie. "He's told me a little about you," she said, "but not much. Tell me about yourself, Donnie. You're, like, a paranormal investigator?"

"Yep, for about two years now. Started slow, but I was lucky enough to get in with a good group of people from the field. Business is great now."

They moved to the living room and sat down while Donnie filled everyone in and answered their questions. They talked about the different types of haunting; residual, where a spirit does something habitually regardless of who is there to witness it; intellectual, when the spirit is purposely interacting with a subject; poltergeist activity; and finally, possession. Then David mentioned the evil character associated with the wooden box again.

"Ah, yes," said Donnie. "The mysterious chest. Where is it?"

"It's over at my house, in Karen's room. Do you want to go get it?"

"Absolutely. Can we go now?"

"Sure," said Jaelyn.

Donnie rose, collecting his equipment. The rest of the group got up with him. When everything was gathered, Donnie looked at the others.

"Let's go get that chest."

CHAPTER 25
THE WARNING

The group arrived at the sorority house. Jaelyn escorted them inside, where some of her sisters eyed the guests curiously. She paused at the bottom of the stairway.

"Her room is up here," said Jaelyn. "Come on." She led Donnie, Lance, and a somewhat hesitant David up the stairs and into Karen's bedroom.

Upon entering the vacant room, Donnie felt something uncomfortable. Not quite a chill, but definitely a vibe that gave him a shiver. Something dark happened here.

His eyes immediately found the wooden chest. Innocently sitting on the corner of Karen's desk, the antique seemed to be beckoning to him. Donnie approached it with wonder, studying the characters carved into the dark wood.

"Look at this," he marveled. "Wow. That's a Haitian soul box."

Jaelyn stepped back. "A what?"

"Yeah, something from their voodoo practices."

Lance was stunned. "Damn, Donnie, you really know your shit."

"Indeed."

Oh my God, how cute, thought Jaelyn, noting Donnie's response being something that Lance often said. *That's where Lance gets it from.*

Donnie had a theory. "This woman from Louisiana, was she by chance from New Orleans?"

"Could be," said Lance. "But I don't know."

"I think she might've been a voodoo priestess. There's a lot of that religion in New Orleans, originally came from Haitian immigrants. If she was a mambo, she likely cursed Grainger's soul and sealed it in this box."

"But now that the box is open...?" Jaelyn said nervously.

Donnie looked at her. "Yeah. His spirit was freed."

"But it was opened back in Colorado," said David, "so that's where he was freed. Could he have followed us here and had something to do with Karen's death?"

"I suppose. Especially if his spirit is still angry. Taking it out on those he is around." Donnie carefully picked up the chest and covered it with its weathered lid. "I'll hang onto this," he declared, "and find out as much as I can about it."

David wanted to leave. Being in the room where Karen died was affecting him. "Is that all we need?" he asked. "Can we go now?"

"Yes," said Donnie. "This is all I came for."

"Come on, guys." Jaelyn headed for the hallway, David and Lance right on her heels. Donnie gave the room a quick, final glance and then brought up the rear.

Eventually, it was dinner time. The crew went to

a Mexican restaurant to enjoy a Southwestern feast and let Lance and Donnie continue to reconnect. It was nice. The feeling around the table brought on by the brothers reuniting was warm.

It was eight o'clock when Donnie hit a wall. He needed rest. He announced his exhaustion, said his goodbyes to the group and hugged Lance again. Then he drove the van back to his motel.

Donnie sat back in a chair and tried to relax. He was perfectly content with spending the rest of the night watching a movie on the television to carry his mind away. After finding something worth watching, he set the remote on the arm of the chair and tried to devote his attention to the TV.

After a while, however, his thoughts reverted back to his brother. He knew Lance better than anyone. Granted, it had been a couple of years since he had seen him. And going to college certainly changed people to some extent. But Donnie felt in the depths of his soul that the brother he had spent time with here was not entirely Lance. If only he had more information.

Then it dawned on him. He had not yet listened to the voice recording he made earlier. He sprang from the chair, went out to the van, and brought the digital recorder back to his room.

Turning off the TV, Donnie activated the playback button on the recorder. He promptly heard his own voice.

"'If there is a presence in this room, let yourself be known.'"

A chuckle came through the small speaker, faint but deep.

"Holy shit," said Donnie. He stopped the playback, went back to the beginning, and turned the volume up.

"'If there is a presence in this room, let yourself be known.'"

The guttural chuckle.

"'Who is here with us?'"

"'*You don't want to know.*'"

"'Please speak to us; let us know you are here.'"

"'*I'm right behind you.*'"

"'I want you to show us a sign that you are here.'"

"'*I will show you.*'"

There was no more audio before the recording ended. Donnie played it back several times, and each time the spectral voice fascinated him more. He analyzed the conversation. "*Right behind you*" could have meant several precise spots, but one made his skin crawl.

Lance had been standing behind Donnie in that room.

David may have been right about his claim. The evidence was not conclusive, but Donnie had probable cause to suspect the unthinkable: Lance had become a vessel for the spirit of Jack Grainger.

It was overwhelming. Donnie closed his eyes and tried to determine what to do next. He would contact some of his associates in the morning and ask their advice. While contemplating exactly who to call and what to say, mixed with the fatigue of his long day, Donnie drifted off in the chair.

He dreamed he had not moved and was still seated in the motel room. Other than the chair he was in, the room was empty. All the furniture was gone, leaving nothing but bare carpeting.

Something moved next to him, catching his attention. He turned his head to see a black balloon floating in midair. He frowned, confused. Then the balloon began drifting, slowly, toward the ceiling. Donnie followed it with his eyes as it was drawn up to the room's ceiling fan.

The balloon swirled upward in the same direction as the whipping blades. Inevitably it made contact with the fan and popped. Dozens of tiny, crumpled pieces of paper were suddenly scattered around the room.

Curious, Donnie got to his feet and examined the wadded papers one by one. There were names written on each one, looking like they were written with quill and ink. But they were not names he knew. Perhaps they were the names of Jack Grainger's victims. Then Donnie opened one with Lance's name on it, and his heart jumped. The next one contained Jim's name, and the next held David's. The last one revealed the name Donnie dreaded finding the most—his own.

He woke with a start. His eyes snapped open, and he quickly assessed his surroundings. In a few moments, Donnie realized he was in the motel room, surrounded by its familiar furnishings, and no longer inside the bizarre dream. He got out of the chair and stretched.

Out of the corner of his eye, he saw it. Resting in the corner, right next to the bed, was a single piece of crumpled paper. It looked just like one from the dream.

His heart rate quickened. Knowing he had to investigate, Donnie walked to the corner and bent down to pick the wadded paper up. It felt cold. When he opened it to see what was on it, adrenaline made his heart beat even faster.

It was the same piece from his dream with his name inked on it.

CHAPTER 26
NEW INFORMATION

Sheriff Bill Skelton stared blankly into his coffee. He stirred some creamer into it, and his gaze was pulled into the endless swirl left behind in the cup. It reminded him of his murder investigation. A whirlwind going around and around but leading nowhere.

The death of Virgil Moreau perplexed him. There was no motive that he could discover. Virgil had not been very popular with the townspeople of Silver Valley due to his migration there from Louisiana. But nobody in town disliked him enough to kill him. As far as the sheriff knew, anyway.

The last ones to see Virgil alive—that Sheriff Skelton was aware of—were the college kids that rented rooms from the motel owner almost two weeks ago. The sheriff did not want to believe the kids had anything to do with the death, especially since witnesses had placed them somewhere else at the time of the murder.

Still, he had to continue investigating every option. He

had nothing else to go on.

Looking at his wristwatch, he noticed it was just after eleven. That would give him enough time to question a few people around town again before getting himself some lunch. The sheriff donned his hat and sunglasses, ceremoniously wiped his graying mustache, and informed his deputy that he was leaving for a couple of hours.

He boarded his cruiser and started the engine. Debating where to go first, he decided he would start with the gas station on the edge of town. He drove to Main Street and took it to Phil's Conoco.

The sheriff parked on the side of the structure and walked inside. The smell of motor oil greeted him. Seeing the owner in his usual seat behind the counter, the sheriff gave a genial wave of the hand. "Howdy, Phil."

The man acknowledged his long-time friend. "Hey, Bill. What can I do for you?"

"Oh, I'm just out today grasping at straws. Need some help with the Moreau case."

"Still no progress?" The attendant showed concern. "You know we're all a little nervous around here. Especially at night."

"I know, I know. I hate wondering whether the killer is here in town or if they've moved on somewhere. I need to solve this case."

"Yep." Phil took a drink of his Dr. Pepper.

"We're coming up with nothing," the sheriff admitted. "No prints on the murder weapon, except those of the victim. No foreign hair or skin cells on the victim. It's like the killer doesn't exist." Frustrated, he tried to calm his tone. "So I need to ask you again, those college kids who left here that day, are you sure about the time?"

Phil remembered going through the surveillance video with the sheriff before. "Yeah, the timestamp doesn't lie."

The sheriff recalled verifying that the timestamp was set accurately. "Right. I don't think they did it, but they're my closest lead. Are you sure you didn't see or hear them say anything that could help shed some light? Like comments about someone they crossed paths with?"

"I'm sure," said Phil. "The only thing I remember hearing that was unusual was one of the girls talking about finding something to wrap a treasure chest."

"You didn't mention that before."

"It didn't have anything to do with what you were looking for."

Sheriff Skelton shrugged. "I reckon not. Well, all right. Thanks, Phil. Take it easy, and I'll see you around."

"Okay, Bill, have a good one."

The sheriff visited a few of the neighboring shops next. He asked the proprietors and employees the same questions he had been delivering for the last twelve days. Nobody had any new input to offer the lawman.

It was time for lunch. Sheriff Skelton went to his favorite eatery, the Italian restaurant on Main Street. The welcoming aroma of fresh bread, garlic, and sausage invaded his nose. It made him hungrier than he thought he was. He strolled to a table in the center and sat down.

"Hi, Sheriff!" said the waitress when she saw him.

"Howdy, Jeannette." The sheriff watched the short woman walk toward him. She looked sunny and cheerful, as always, with her bright eyes and unmistakable blonde curls.

"What can I get you today?" she asked while filling his water glass.

He thought for a moment. "I think the meatball sandwich."

"Alrighty, can't go wrong with that."

"I want to talk for just a minute if you don't mind."

"Sure," Jeannette permitted. "What's on your mind?"

"It's those college kids," the sheriff began. "You know, a couple of weeks ago. They were here the weekend Virgil Moreau was killed."

"Yes, I remember. You asked me a lot of questions about them."

"Yep. I know I did, but I have to ask you again. Is there anything at all you can tell me about them?"

Jeannette gazed down at the table, stirring her memory. "Like I said, they were just your average, goofy college kids. Fun, happy. And excited. They had come all the way up here from ASU to see the ghost lights. They wanted me to go with them, but I told them I'd had my share of searching that field."

"Searching?"

"Yeah, we got to talking about how I'd seen the lights since I was a kid. And how we'd all go out during the day digging for treasure. I told them about the legend of Black Jack's treasure and that it was supposed to be buried somewhere in the field."

The sheriff raised an eyebrow. "Black Jack?"

"Oh, it's just an old legend my grandfather told me about when I was a kid."

Sheriff Skelton leaned back with a wrinkled brow.

"You mean Jack Grainger." He clearly knew something about the legend.

"Oh my God, you know about it? I thought my grandfather made it up."

"No, my dear, it's a real person. One of the most evil characters of the Old West." He tapped his finger on the tablecloth. "And he died right here in Silver Valley."

Jeannette's eyes widened. "Did he really have a treasure?"

The sheriff chuckled. "No, afraid not. His remains were buried out there, but definitely no treasure." His smile instantly vanished, remembering what the gas station attendant had told him. "Unless his remains were inside a treasure chest...."

"Huh?"

"Nothing, dear. Just thinking aloud."

"Oh. I'll get your sandwich out here in a jiffy." She turned and headed for the kitchen.

"Thank you, Jeannette."

The sheriff leaned back and reflected. He remembered hearing, many years ago, about the legend of Jack Grainger. There was definitely something about a wooden chest. A rumor that Grainger's murderer used witchcraft to kill him and curse his remains inside the box.

Had the college students unearthed that elusive chest? *No*, he scoffed at himself, *don't be stupid. That's just old urban legend, nonsense.*

Sheriff Skelton sipped his water while waiting for his lunch to arrive.

CHAPTER 27
DREAMSPEAK

"That doesn't mean anything."

Donnie's eyes were locked on the EMF meter. The LED display was in the red. "Um, it means you've got some abnormal waves coming out of you."

"Told you," said David. "Possessed."

Lance rolled his eyes. "Is possession even what that piece of equipment is designed to detect?"

"Well, not exactly," Donnie confessed. "It's for reading electromagnetic frequencies. But in my field, we use this to find spirit activity."

"Besides," said Lance, "even if I *was* possessed, I'm not now. Maybe you're just reading the leftovers."

David chortled at the statement. "Leftovers. Nice."

Donnie shrugged. "You might be right." He would have to give his brother the benefit of the doubt. But in the back of his mind, he still felt that the person before him was not entirely his brother. Donnie would keep a watchful eye on him. "Let's get the camera from next door and see what we got."

David fervently agreed. "Hell yeah." He grabbed his neighbor's spare key from the wall hook. The group traipsed to the next unit over.

David unlocked the door to Jim's apartment. The trio of men entered, heading straight for the full-spectrum camcorder Donnie had set up there. It was still running, which was good. There would be an entire day's worth of video to go through.

They brought the gear back to Lance's place. Donnie plugged the camcorder into Lance's television to watch the playback on the big screen. David nestled into the couch, eager to see the results.

Jim's apartment came into view on the TV. Donnie had the camera in thermal mode, so anything that was room temperature was dark. He manned the remote to scan forward. The group's eyes were glued to the screen. The timestamp churned forward in the bottom right corner as the men watched diligently. No activity was visible, however; the camcorder had caught nothing.

"That's disappointing," Donnie moped. "I was hoping there was still spirit activity in that room."

"Guess not," said Lance. He looked at David. "Either Jim's ritual did the trick, or you guys were just crazy to begin with."

David dropped his head. "And Jim almost died."

"Hey," said Donnie, recognizing the need for a distraction, "what do you say we find something fun to do today?"

"It's hot as hell outside," Lance remarked. It was over a

hundred degrees in the sun, which was normal for the desert in summer.

"So let's go do something indoors. What do you have around here that's cool?"

"Well," said Lance, "I haven't seen the aquarium yet. It's not far, and I hear it's pretty cool."

Donnie smiled. "Sounds like a winner. Let's go do it."

"Can we bring Jaelyn?" asked Lance. "I'm sure she'd love to come along."

"Absolutely. Call her up and tell her to get her butt over here. Then we head out."

The group took Lance's car. They spent a few hours enjoying Sea Life Aquarium, found a nice place to have dinner, and then stopped somewhere for a few beers.

At the end of the busy day with Lance and his friends, Donnie returned to his motel room for the night. It only took an hour of television to make him tired enough to go to sleep. He brushed his teeth, turned off the TV, and went to bed.

Donnie dreamed he was standing in a vast field. The sun was high in the sky, but the light it gave was dim. A small dust devil danced toward him, swirling dirt and sand in a cyclonic pattern. It paused in front of Donnie and remained rooted there. Then a voice came from inside the column of hot air.

"*Why are you here?*" it asked. The voice was deep, gritty; it sounded like the same voice Donnie had captured on the digital recorder.

"I'm here for my brother," Donnie replied matter-of-factly.

"*Let him take care of himself.*"

"I can't do that."

"You're wasting your time."

Donnie's eyes opened. He was awake in the bed, staring upward in the dark. Not knowing how long he had been asleep, he looked at the nightstand clock. It was already eleven.

What a strange dream, he reflected. The eerie scene was fresh in his mind. He analyzed the conversation and concluded that it had to be more than just a dream. The man speaking to him must have been the villain his brother and David were talking about.

Donnie wanted more information. If he could engage in further dreamspeak with this entity, perhaps he could discover its intentions. Donnie closed his eyes and tried to get back to sleep.

Eventually, he found himself in the open field once more. The whirlwind was still loitering in front of him, swaying like a serpent. Donnie resumed the dialogue. "Who are you?"

The dust devil was silent.

"Who are you?" Donnie repeated. "Don't be afraid."

"I'm not afraid," the voice said.

"Neither am I," said Donnie. "You're Jack Grainger, aren't you?"

There was a pause. *"You have no reason to help Lance."*

"Of course I do."

"Why should you wish to help him?"

"He needs my help."

"You have no reason to help him," the voice proclaimed. *"He already has everything."*

"What do you mean?"

"*Mom and Dad have given him everything, and you nothing.*"

"That's not Lance's fault. That's between my parents and me."

"*He's been given everything while you've received nothing but scorn.*"

Donnie knew that was true. But he still had no reason to hold that against his brother.

"*Don't you hate the spoiled little brat?*" said the voice, trying to drive the divisive wedge.

It was working. He thought of all the times he was disregarded, shunned, and spurned while his brother was treated like precious royalty. Donnie started to feel his soul turning angry.

"*Let me in.*"

It was wrong. Something inside Donnie knew he was being manipulated. He quickly shook the negative suggestions off. "No. *No!* He's my brother."

"*Let me in—*"

A sound woke Donnie.

Ears perked. He listened for it. He heard it again. A rattling sound, like someone trying to open the door to his room. The lock prevented entry. A calm knocking on the door followed.

Who the fuck could that be? thought Donnie. He kept quiet, hoping the unwelcome visitor would go away.

The knocking persisted. Quiet, steady, patient.

Donnie continued to ignore the rapping. Maybe it was just a drunk trying to solicit the wrong room. It had to be;

nobody that could be looking for Donnie knew where he was staying. Except for Lance.

"*Let me in*" still lingered from the dream. Suddenly Donnie had a terrifying feeling.

What if it was his brother on the other side of that door?

Or, more specifically, what if it was someone else in his brother's body? Wearing him, like a uniform and coming over to deal with Donnie? With dead eyes and a broad, sinister grin?

Donnie shuddered at the disturbing thought. He remained perfectly still on the mattress and completely quiet. He barely breathed until whoever was knocking finally gave up and went away.

CHAPTER 28
VISITING HOURS

It was a cloudy Saturday morning, which did not help the group's somber mood. Thinking about their friend Jim, they wanted to swing by Tempe St. Luke's to visit him. They had already stopped by the hospital a couple of times since his episode to check on his condition, but he had not been awake to receive them. Jim was stable, though, which was something.

David checked in with the receptionist to ask to see Jim. The clerk notified one of the nurses that the patient had visitors who wanted to see him. The doctor came out a few minutes later to talk to the group.

"Hello, all," she said, recognizing everybody but Donnie. "He's still sedated, but he's doing okay."

"That's good, I guess," David sighed. "I just wish he was awake to talk to us."

"I know," said the doctor. "Give him time. He'll get there. He seems like a fighter."

"He is," Jaelyn affirmed. "He'll pull through this. I'm sure of it."

The physician smiled. "You just missed his parents. They left about half an hour ago. Jim is lucky to have his family and friends care so much about him."

"Can we see him?" asked Lance. "We won't disturb him."

"Yes, I think that would be okay," the doctor allowed. "But just for a little while. He'll be due for meds soon. And just two at a time, okay?"

Donnie was content staying in the waiting room, and Lance hung back with him. David and Jaelyn went with the doctor and navigated the hallway to Jim's room. Remembering the way from last time, they knew exactly where they were going.

Jim was unconscious in his bed, his body wrapped in bandages that looked like they had been recently changed. Jaelyn's heart sank when she saw their motionless friend. She stepped up to the bed, and David followed. They sat down.

"How're you doing, you crazy Indian?" David said softly.

"Hey, Jim," said Jaelyn. "They said you're gonna be okay. Do you hear me? Just keep fighting and get better." Her throat tightened as her emotions got the best of her.

David stared at his wretched neighbor. The young man looked unnatural, almost dead. The color had returned to his skin, for the most part, but there was no life in his face. David understood what Jim had gone through, so his appearance was not shocking. But still, it was hard to see Jim like this.

"We're here, buddy," David stated to medicated ears.

"If you can hear me, know that we love ya." He held Jim's hand to let him know someone was with him. Jim's skin felt spongy, clammy.

David suddenly began to weep. He felt horrible about the traumatic events. Why had this happened to Jim? He had done nothing to deserve this. All he wanted to do was help. And as a result, he almost shredded himself to death.

Jaelyn placed her hand on David's shoulder, which prompted him to sob harder. "It's okay," she whispered to him. He needed to get it out. After a minute, he was able to collect himself and draw in a fortifying breath.

"You got this, buddy," David said to the sleeping patient. "You're tough. We know you're gonna get better. No matter how long it takes." The Latino smirked. "You're Indian Jim, goddamnit."

Jaelyn grinned. "That's right."

David leaned closer to Jim's ear. "Whatever's going on with Lance and this ghost, we're gonna beat it. All of us. Together. I'll damn sure see to that, Jim."

A nurse arrived a short while later. She ushered the visitors aside so she could administer the medication to the IV. Then she politely sent them out, stating it was time for Jim to have some quiet rest.

***

The group left the hospital and walked back to Lance's apartment. They went inside to escape the August heat. Finding a good baseball game to watch on TV, they sat down to unwind. After a while, they decided to order pizzas.

Donnie had been thinking about why he was there and how he might need to work on his brother. But so far, Lance had not exhibited any peculiar behavior. All seemed normal. Donnie elected to enjoy his time with Lance. But he would still keep a discreet eye on him.

Since it was Saturday night, Lance announced he wanted to go out to the bars near campus. Jaelyn thought that would be a nice distraction for them, and Donnie was okay with that as well.

But David did not feel like going anywhere. "You all go without me," he directed. "I think I just want to stay home and turn in early."

"Are you sure?" said Jaelyn.

"Yeah. Just not in the mood. Sorry."

"That's okay," Donnie said. "Hope you feel better later."

"Thanks," nodded David. "Now go on, kids, get out of here and have some fun."

The others left, and David had the quiet apartment to himself. He found a comedy on the television, something to take his mind off Jim. It worked, for the most part, and David's mind was soon focused on the entertaining movie.

David tired early. By nine o'clock, he was ready for bed. Turning off the TV, he walked to the bathroom to brush his teeth. Then he shuffled to his bedroom and shut the door.

He undressed, flicked the light switch off, and got into bed. He lay there for a while, staring upward at nothing. There was so much on his mind that it was hard to drift off. But he closed his eyes and tried.

Suddenly he heard the sound of a reptile hissing.

His eyes snapped open, darting in the dark. Had a rattlesnake found its way inside the apartment? David listened intently. He could hear the smooth sound of something sliding across the bedroom floor. Fear jolting him, he quickly sat up and turned the bedside lamp on.

There was no snake on the floor. Just the wooden desk chair, although not quite where he remembered it being.

Afraid something might have gone under the bed, David dropped one of his pillows over the edge of the bed. Nothing attacked it. He tossed the other pillow on top of the first one. After no reaction, he tentatively set his feet on the pillows and got out of bed. Then, slowly, he bent down to see what was beneath.

Nothing.

David sighed in relief. He returned to his bed and leaned over to turn the light off. Out of the corner of his eye, he saw the chair move slightly. He froze and faced the chair.

The wooden chair came apart. It split everywhere along the grain and untwisted into long, thin pieces. Spindles separated from the back frame and coiled up like snakes. Then the entire chair melted to the floor in a pile of squirming serpents.

"*Jesus!*" David exclaimed, shrinking back into his pillows. His brain could barely comprehend what his eyes were seeing. He was powerless to move as he watched the slender, slithering things move toward the bed.

Then his bedposts transformed into thick snakes, their glassy eyes quickly fixed on David. His heart was pounding. The four corners swayed like ominous guards, daring him to move.

Suddenly he saw long, translucent fangs burst out from the side of his pillow. The pillow then began closing around his head. David's hands flew to the ends of the pillow to stop it, but it was too strong. His pillow had become the cottony mouth of a huge viper, and it had him.

Unable to peel it open, David screamed insanely.

CHAPTER 29
RETREAT

Nothing anybody could say was going to change his mind. After the terrifying night he had endured, David knew it was time to distance himself from the situation.

He had fled his bedroom last night and cowered on the couch until morning. Only in the light of day did David feel safe enough to return to his room. Now he was packing whatever he could into his two suitcases.

Lance stood in the kitchen while using his phone. He called Donnie and Jaelyn, informing them of David's intentions. Each of them announced they would be right over.

When they arrived, Lance let them inside the apartment. Jaelyn gave Lance a quick kiss, then went straight for David's room. She saw him stuffing the suitcases, and she placed her hands on her hips.

"David Lucero," she scolded, "just where do you think you're going?"

He turned to face her, and she saw genuine fear in his

eyes. "I have to get away from here," he stated. "I can't stay. I'm next."

"What?"

He stepped closer to her. "Last night, I was attacked. Here! In my bedroom."

"My God! Who...?"

"The fucking ghost!" David said. "Turned my bed into snakes. *Snakes*, for God's sake!"

Jaelyn was speechless. All she could do was look at David.

"It almost suffocated me with my own pillow. I'm sorry...I want to help and all, but I'm not sticking around to end up like Jim. Or worse, like Todd or Karen."

The statement dazed Jaelyn. She moved aside as David brought the suitcases out of his room and plopped them on the floor behind the couch.

"Where are you going?" enquired Donnie.

"Back home. Nathan's picking me up and taking me to the airport."

"Just like that?"

"Dude, you have no idea what actually happened to me last night. Everything in my room turned into something that wanted to kill me."

"Okay...." Donnie was not sure if David had been the victim of a supernatural attack or if the Latino had simply gone crazy.

"I gotta get out of here. I'm going back to Pueblo to be safe at home with my parents. I'm sorry. I just can't take it anymore." He turned his eyes to Lance. "I'm sorry," he repeated.

Lance did not reply. He merely stood in the kitchen with his eyes closed, rubbing the side of his neck.

"Listen, David," said Donnie. "Whatever you think you saw, you can't let it get to you. We all need to stick together here."

"I can't. I just...can't."

The beep of a car horn was heard — David's ride was here. He grabbed his gear and left the apartment. The others followed him outside to the balcony.

They watched David lug his suitcases down the steps and to the waiting Toyota. He gave a final, apologetic wave to his friends. Then he got in, and the vehicle drove away, heading for Sky Harbor International.

The three stayed on the balcony, reflecting on the morning's unexpected events. Donnie and Lance looked at each other.

"You didn't say much to try to stop him," noted Donnie.

Lance shrugged. "What was I going to say? The same things you two did? And we see how well that worked."

"Still...."

"He wasn't going to change his mind, Donnie. I tried to talk some sense into him before I called you, but he had already decided to run away. And I'm okay with that."

"You are?" asked Jaelyn, concerned.

"Yeah. I mean, I understand he needs to go home. He'll figure himself out."

Donnie frowned. He once again had the feeling that Lance was not quite himself. Perhaps he was still afflicted with the parasitic spirit after all. Donnie would need to pursue options for saving his brother.

"Are you okay?" Jaelyn said, wrapping her arm around Lance's waist.

"Yeah, I'm fine."

"I can't believe he just up and left," she marveled. "I mean, *poof.*"

The slightest grin curled up the side of Lance's mouth. "*Poof.*"

"Well, I'm not leaving you," she stated, giving him a kiss on the cheek. "We'll figure out what's going on here."

Donnie stared at his sibling with firm eyes. "I'm not going anywhere either, little brother," he vowed.

CHAPTER 30
A BIG FAVOR

The mood was somber. The shock of David's unexpected departure still had its hold on the group. To dispel the gloom, Lance turned on the television. The chatter of the morning news helped, providing a smidgen of normalcy. The group sat in the living room and quietly watched the broadcast.

After an hour of awkward silence, Jaelyn spoke up. "Let's get out of here," she suggested. "Find something else to do."

"Like what?" said Lance.

"Let's go see a movie."

Donnie raised his eyebrows. "That's not a bad idea. Why don't the two of you go out, enjoy some time together, and I'll hang back here?"

"Don't be silly," Jaelyn said. "You come with us."

"No, I need to stay behind and do some work researching stuff. Go on," he reassured, "and I'll see you both when you get back."

"Okay," shrugged Jaelyn. She tugged at Lance. "Come on, you; let's go find a fun movie to watch." Lance grumbled a bit but complied with his girlfriend's wishes. They said goodbye to Donnie and disappeared out the door.

Now that Donnie was alone, he had a chance to contemplate his next move. Something was clearly inhabiting his brother and still tormenting those around him. He thought about an exorcism but had doubts. It was the spirit of a man, not a demon, possessing Lance. Donnie spent half an hour online searching for anything useful to their predicament. Then, finding nothing substantial, he decided to try asking some of his business contacts.

Donnie opened his list of contacts and found Greg Thomson. Greg, a renowned scientist who had spent the last thirty years studying parapsychology and paranormal activity, was introduced to Donnie during a joint investigation of a major presence at an abandoned sanitarium in Texas. Greg took to the ambitious newcomer and taught him quite a lot during the one-week study. If anybody could shed some much-needed light on Donnie's task, it would be Greg.

He tapped the button to call, and Greg's phone rang. After a few rings, the elder man answered. "Hello?"

"Hi, is this Greg?"

"Yes," the man replied. "And is this young Donnie?" Obviously, the man still had Donnie's contact information saved on his phone's caller ID.

"It is indeed," said Donnie, a smile forming on his face. "How are you doing, sir?"

"I'm well, thank you," Greg replied. He sensed that this was not a social call and waited for Donnie to announce his reason for calling.

"Glad to hear. Hey, listen, I'm currently in the middle of a situation that has me stumped."

The scientist was intrigued. "How can I help?"

"I think I may have a problem involving possession."

"Really? Tell me."

"My younger brother and his friends from ASU were in an old mining town in Colorado. They were there to see ghost lights."

"Silver Valley?"

Donnie was taken aback a little. "Yeah. You've apparently heard of it."

"I have heard of the lights up there. Always wanted to check it out for myself."

"Well, while they were chasing them around the field, they found a wooden chest that had been buried there. But when they opened it, it was full of live bugs. Palmetto bugs, according to one of them."

"In Colorado?" scoffed Greg. "That's a Southern insect."

"You're right," Donnie affirmed before explaining. "Turns out this chest was supposedly the resting place for the remains of a bad, bad dude. Someone named Jack Grainger. Killed a lot of people during the cowboy days. The woman who put his remains in the chest was, I believe, a voodoo priestess from New Orleans. One of the places palmetto bugs come from."

"Hmm."

"I've got the chest," stated Donnie. "It appears to be a Haitian soul box."

"I assume there was a spirit in that chest who is now the cause of your problem?"

"Yep. We think this Grainger is possessing my brother."

"In cases like that, the spirit is always after the one who releases it. There's a type of bond there."

"Then why is it haunting and hurting everyone *else* from the group? Tragic things have been happening to those around us. And I've had some experiences with the spirit as well."

"Ah, because they are a potential threat to the spirit's intentions."

"Because they might get in the way?"

"Exactly. It will confuse and frighten them. It needs to break them down emotionally, weaken them." Greg cleared his throat. "And in some cases, harm them."

Donnie nodded. "There have been a couple of deaths involved up here."

"My God."

"Yeah. It's serious."

"But ultimately, the spirit has no interest in any others. It always intended on occupying the one who released it."

"There's just one problem with that," said Donnie.

Greg knew. "That person is your brother."

"Exactly." Donnie released a heavy breath. "Since I got here, I've taken some hot EMF readings and made voice recordings where I've heard the bad entity's voice on the playback. My brother's roommate said a neighbor even tried an Indian ritual to expel the spirit, but I don't think it worked. And that neighbor is now in the hospital fighting for his life after nearly bleeding to death after scratching phantasmic bugs. It's crazy up here. So I'm not sure what to do next, Greg. I need you to tell me how to resolve this situation."

Greg was quiet for a moment. "You really got yourself a doozie there, Donnie," Greg admitted after processing everything he had just heard. "Let me do some research and confer with some others. Then I'll get back to you. Okay?"

"Okay. Soon as you can. Thanks, Greg."

"My pleasure, young man. Talk to you soon." Greg ended the call.

Now Donnie could only hope his reputable associate would find the solution to Lance's ailment. He had to wait by the phone, and it would probably take a while. The time dragged on, each minute feeling like ten.

Finally, almost two hours later, Donnie's phone rang. He was in the kitchen, rummaging through the refrigerator for something to snack on, when he heard the ringer. His eyes jumped to the display, hopeful that it was Greg calling him back. Thankfully it was.

"Hello, Greg," Donnie greeted. "Any luck?"

"Are you sitting down?"

Donnie felt his adrenaline building as he detected urgency. "Something tells me I need to be," said Donnie, returning to the couch. "Hit me."

"Here's what you're gonna do. I got hold of Brooke Danforth, whom I trust with my life. She is familiar with the history of Silver Valley and knows people there. She's made arrangements for you to bring your brother to the Amish in Silver Valley for help."

"The *Amish?*" blurted Donnie, surprised. "How can *they* help?"

"You have to trust me. Brooke wouldn't lead me wrong. She says you need to bring your brother to them for two reasons. One, the Amish can perform an exorcism ritual that could free your brother from this spirit. And two, that's the area the spirit needs to be returned to."

"What would the Amish know about exorcisms?"

"You'd be surprised. After all, the Amish religion was created from Swiss Anabaptism, which came from Protestantism, which was a split from Catholicism. They all believe in Jesus, after all, who was well known for performing exorcisms, particularly in the Gospels of Matthew and Mark."

Donnie considered this. "Okay, I guess they might know something about exorcisms. So, what do I do now? Where do I go?"

"Take him to Silver Valley," Greg reiterated. "Just past town is a dirt road that will take you to the Amish community. They'll be waiting for you."

Donnie's head was spinning from the weight of everything on his shoulders. But he would try anything to make his brother well, even if it meant another long road trip. "Okay then. I guess we'll hit the highway tomorrow morning. Thanks again, Greg. You're a lifesaver—I owe you big."

"Happy to be able to help," Greg said softly. "You just take care of your brother. And best of luck to you, Donnie."

CHAPTER 31
THE JOURNEY

Donnie pulled into the apartment building complex and parked his van. Picking up the bag from the passenger seat, he stepped out and walked to Lance's door. He knocked lightly, hoping his brother was not still sleeping.

He heard the lock disengage, and then the door opened. Jaelyn stood in the entryway. "Mornin', Donnie," she said, yawning. "We just woke up. Come on in."

"I brought breakfast," Donnie announced. He placed the bag on the counter and reached inside. He pulled out a handful of foil-wrapped burritos. "Egg and cheese breakfast burritos, some with chorizo."

"Awesome," said Jaelyn. "Want some coffee?"

"Absolutely."

Lance turned his head from his position on the couch. "I'm not hungry," he stated, "but thanks."

Jaelyn handed Donnie a steaming cup. "What brings you over so early?"

Donnie wandered to the living room, and Jaelyn accompanied him. He was not sure how to begin. "Well, I talked to a friend yesterday and told him about our situation. Told him everything that's happened."

Lance frowned. "Yeah?"

"Yeah, and he has a way to help us. But it's gonna be a long road trip. So I figured the earlier we left, the better."

"Road trip to where?" asked Jaelyn.

"Silver Valley, where you found that chest."

"Are you kidding?" scoffed Lance. "That's stupid. Why would we go there?"

Donnie cleared his throat. The words he was about to speak were difficult. "Well, arrangements have been made to cleanse you of any invading spirit that might be in you."

Jaelyn was excited by the announcement. "Really? What kind of arrangements?"

The idea of an Amish exorcism would not be received well. "Probably best I leave it as a surprise," said Donnie.

Lance rubbed the side of his neck. "I'm not going back there," he avowed.

"Come on, Lance," Jaelyn said, touching his shoulder. "It'll help you. Let's go."

At once, Lance's eyes turned murky, one darker than the other. Almost black.

Jaelyn recoiled. The young man before her suddenly felt like a stranger to her; this was not Lance. Her heart skipped a beat when he spoke.

"I will not go back to that place!" an alien voice said. It was deep, guttural.

Donnie knew that voice. It was the same voice from the digital recording, the same voice from his dreams. But witnessing it coming from the mouth of his brother jarred him.

Nevertheless, Donnie stiffened. "You *are* going back to that place, and I'm taking you." He stepped closer to Lance.

The room went cold.

Donnie and Jaelyn felt the chill immediately. It was as if they had just walked into a meat locker. Sensing something sinister in the room, they froze and looked nervously at each other.

Lance erupted from the couch. With shocking speed, he turned on his brother and grabbed him by the throat. Jaelyn shrieked.

"You were stupid to stay here!" the voice bellowed. "You should've left when you had the chance! Now you're gonna have to die!"

The grip was strong. Donnie felt his eyes bulging. He struck at his brother's arm but could not break Lance's grasp. "Lance…," he croaked.

"He's *mine!*" hissed the voice. "You hear me? *Mine!*" Lance's eyes were shiny with rage.

"…Stop…."

"I'll kill anybody that stands in my way!"

"*Stop it!*" Jaelyn screamed. She could see the sheer terror in Donnie's eyes as he was being choked. "Lance, let go of him!"

Lance ignored her. He kept his gaze fixed on the face of his victim, his lips curled into a wry smile.

"Stop it!" she insisted. She grabbed Lance's hand and tried to pry it from Donnie's neck. The steel grip would not be weakened. Lance angrily gripped Jaelyn's arm with his free hand and flung her across the room. She stumbled and hit the floor with a hard smack.

Jaelyn had to do something—something drastic. Spotting the ornate granite bowl on the table, she picked it up. She held it tightly and swung it at Lance, striking him in the left temple. Lance lost consciousness. He went limp and collapsed to the floor. Donnie fell with him. Freed of Lance's hand, Donnie sucked air back into his body.

Jaelyn was trembling. "Ohmygod, ohmygod," she stammered. "Did I...? Is he...?"

Donnie leaned over and examined his brother. "He's still breathing. You just knocked him out. He'll be okay."

"Are *you* all right?"

"The room's still spinning, but yeah. I'm okay."

Jaelyn looked around nervously. "We aren't safe with him anymore. We have to do something."

"We need to get him up to Silver Valley," Donnie reaffirmed. "Like right away. But we'll have to find a way to keep him sedated for the journey."

Jaelyn had a possible solution. "I'm going back to the house," she said. "One of my sorority sisters, Ginger, is pre-med. She should be able to get us some tranquilizers."

"We're gonna need something stronger than Xanax or Valium, I'm afraid."

"I know. We'll need some anti-aggression sedatives."

Donnie raised an eyebrow. "You think your friend can get her hands on something like that?"

Jaelyn fidgeted. "She's kinda...with the professor. It's complicated."

Donnie chuckled. "On the contrary, it's pretty simple.

Say no more."

"All right, I'll be back as quickly as I can."

"Okay. I'll keep him here."

Jaelyn glanced at her unconscious boyfriend once more. Then she slipped her shoes on, grabbed her purse, and hurried to the sorority house.

Donnie massaged his throat while figuring out what to do next. The first thing he needed to do, he supposed, was to confine Lance so he could not hurt anybody. Donnie did a quick search through the apartment, hoping to find some rope, zip ties, or even duct tape. Nothing of the sort. He had to think of something fast before Lance came to.

He spotted an extension cord in the corner, behind the entertainment center. *That'll work*, he deduced. He scampered to the corner, unplugged the cord, and brought it to Lance's body. Then Donnie hoisted his brother onto a chair and tied him securely to it.

Convinced that Lance was unable to move, Donnie's next goal was to keep Lance quiet. He found a T-shirt in Lance's bedroom and a small washcloth in the kitchen that could be used to gag him. He packed the washcloth into Lance's mouth, making sure his brother could breathe through his nose. Then he strung the shirt across Lance's mouth and tied it behind his neck.

Lance's eyes opened. They were still not his eyes. After a second of realization, Lance furiously fought to free himself. His struggling was futile; Donnie had bound him thoroughly.

"Just relax," Donnie said to the anger inside his brother. "You can't move, and no one outside this apartment can hear you. So just try to settle down."

Lance's eyes burned with fury. He grumbled something into his stuffed mouth.

"I know you're in there, Lance," said Donnie. "I know it wasn't you that was trying to kill me. You need to fight him. You can't let him take you over, Lance."

Lance merely stared at Donnie audaciously.

Donnie could only gaze back, conveying two messages with his eyes: that he was there for his brother and that he was not afraid of the entity within.

Jaelyn's sorority sister dropped her off in the parking lot a little over an hour later. Carrying a small suitcase, Jaelyn trotted up the steps to Lance's apartment. She entered and brought the suitcase to the living room.

Donnie was relieved to see her. The time spent alone with his altered brother had been an emotional strain on him. Finally, he had reinforcements back with him. "Any luck?" he asked her.

Jaelyn nodded. "Oh yeah." She opened her suitcase to reveal a bunch of syringes on top of her traveling clothes and toiletries. "We have enough here to keep him sedated for several days."

"What's in them?"

"Ginger calls it 'the cocktail.' It's a mix of Haldol, Ativan, and Benadryl."

It sounded less potent than Donnie had hoped for. "That's gonna knock him out?" he said with worried skepticism.

"Yep," Jaelyn assured. "The combination of the three will definitely do the trick. She says to give him one every six hours, or as needed depending on his…behavior."

"It won't be easy," Donnie admitted. "He's not going to hold still for us."

"If you can hold him, I can give him a shot in the leg."

"Okay," said Donnie. "Let's try it." He turned to face his brother in the chair. "Hang in there, Lance. We're gonna fix you."

Lance watched Jaelyn ready one of the syringes and approach him. His voice spat unrecognizable outbursts into the gag. Veins of anger bulged on his forehead.

Donnie knelt on the floor before him. He nodded to Jaelyn and wrapped his arms tightly around Lance's legs. Lance bucked immediately, but Donnie was able to hold him steady enough for Jaelyn to administer a shot to Lance's thigh. Lance roared from behind the cloth muzzle.

Within minutes, Lance's muddy eyes became glazed. Then they appeared to get clearer, brighter. They looked like Lance's eyes again just before his eyelids closed. He was knocked out.

Relief swept Donnie and Jaelyn. They both exhaled deeply and stood back. Watching the motionless young man in the chair, they knew it was time to get everybody in the van and on the road.

Donnie went to Lance's bedroom. He pulled some of Lance's clothes from the dresser and brought them out to the living room. He thrust them into a plastic bag. "I'm not sure how long we're gonna be there," said Donnie, "but this should be enough for him to change into, as he needs to."

Jaelyn nodded. "I brought what I thought I'd need for myself," she stated, motioning toward her suitcase.

"You want me to take that down to the van for you?"

asked Donnie. "I'm loading up now, and then the last thing we'll do is bring Lance down."

"Okay. I'll keep an eye on him while you go."

Donnie grabbed the suitcase and the plastic bag. Then he took them outside and down the stairs to the parking lot. He returned to the apartment minutes later.

"Now we just have to get Lance down there," said Donnie. "Come on. I'll untie him, and then we'll each take a side and walk him."

Jaelyn held Lance upright while Donnie loosened the extension cord. Then the two of them lifted Lance by his armpits and brought him to the door.

"Okay," said Donnie. "Look outside and see if anyone's out there."

Jaelyn opened the door and scouted. There were no nosy witnesses anywhere to be seen. "The coast is clear," she claimed.

They each took an arm and carried Lance out of the apartment and down the concrete steps. Donnie was nervous about being seen. He quickened their pace to the van.

Once Lance was laid in the back, Donnie once again bound him with the extension cord. Then he started the vehicle and drove away. He only had one more stop to make before they hit the highway. Donnie parked at the motel he was staying in to retrieve his belongings.

"All right," he stated, "I'll be back in a flash."

"And don't forget the wooden chest," said Jaelyn.

"Ah. No, we don't want to forget that."

Donnie walked to his room and used his key card to unlock the door. Then he entered the room, packed up all of his belongings, and brought everything out to the van. He placed the old chest inside his steel cabinet and locked it. Then he jogged to the office to check out and settle his bill.

Donnie drove them out of Tempe, onto I-40, and followed the highway northeast. As the city faded behind them and all that surrounded the van was sand and brush, the travelers felt a little safer. Now all they had to do was obey the speed limit and stay alert in order to avoid accidents.

"So tell me," said Jaelyn. "What exactly are we gonna do in Silver Valley?"

"You'll think I'm nuts, but we're going to see the Amish for help."

Jaelyn thought she had misheard him. "The Amish?"

"Yeah, I know. But you have to believe me, it's gonna work. My friend Greg contacted somebody up there that was able to make arrangements with the Amish. And they've agreed to do an exorcism ritual on Lance."

"Wow," was all she could say. But she did not doubt anything he told her.

The scenery changed from flat desert to hills laden with pine trees. Jaelyn checked on Lance every so often to make sure he was still restrained and sedated. After four hours, Lance began to stir. Jaelyn hastily went to her suitcase and procured another syringe. She unscrewed the Luer lock to expose the needle, pressed the plunger enough to expel any air from the tip, and injected the medication into Lance's arm.

Eventually, it was time for a restroom stop. Spotting a rest area ahead, Donnie slowed down to pull off. He parked as close to the facility as he could. He looked over at his partner. "You want to go first?"

"We can both go at the same time," she suggested.

"And leave him unattended?"

"He's not going anywhere."

"I know, but I don't want to take a chance that someone looks inside the van while we're both gone."

Jaelyn's eyes broadened with understanding. "Good point."

"After all, this is technically kidnapping. Especially since we'll be taking him across state lines."

"Okay, I'll go first," said Jaelyn. She hopped out of the van and wandered inside the ladies' room. When she had finished, she emerged from the structure and jumped back into the van. Then she took her turn guarding while Donnie went inside to relieve himself.

The hours were wearisome. They stopped a few times for gas, bathroom breaks, and food to go. By the time they reached the New Mexico border, it was already three o'clock. And their journey was not even half over.

They passed the time by talking. Jaelyn and Donnie learned a great deal about each other. Donnie was pleased that his brother had found someone with such a good heart. And Jaelyn had a better understanding of what life in the Bowser household was like for the two boys growing up.

The sunset over the southern Sangre de Cristo Mountains was stunning. The lucid oranges and pinks blanketed the New Mexico sky as the sun retired. Donnie had to turn on the van's headlights as he continued toward Colorado. Jaelyn checked on Lance's condition, gave him another dose, and returned to the passenger seat to sleep for a while.

It was well past eleven when they finally saw the small town of Silver Valley.

CHAPTER 32
HUMBLE GUESTS

The wide valley was black at night. The lights of Silver Valley were a lone beacon for the van. Donnie followed the winding road down the side of the range and into the small town.

"So this is it," said Donnie. "Where did you all see the ghost lights?"

"Out there a ways," Jaelyn replied, pointing to the left. "In the field past an old church."

There were no other cars on Main Street at this time of night. "I can't believe how quiet it is," said Donnie. "Not a single car out."

"It *is* a small town," Jaelyn pointed out.

"I know, but not even any other travelers coming through? I figured we'd have more cover."

"What do you mean?"

"I was hoping we would just be one of many vehicles passing through, so we wouldn't be noticed. But we're the only car out. We stick out like a sore thumb."

"So what? Nobody's looking for us."

Donnie's eyes scanned the street as he drove. "I'm still worried about running into local cops. We need to avoid the police at all costs."

Jaelyn agreed. "True. But just stay below the speed limit, and we'll be fine."

"I suppose...."

"Besides, we're almost through the town."

They passed the sleeping shops, restaurants, and a bar whose lights indicated it was open. Upon reaching the edge of town, Donnie's heart skipped a beat when he saw a police car parked on the side of the road.

"Oh shit," he murmured. He quickly glanced in the rearview mirror to make sure Lance was still unconscious.

Jaelyn steadied him. "Be cool. Just drive like normal."

Donnie's pulse was racing. He knew that if the police discovered Lance in the back, Donnie would likely be going to prison. He drove past the dormant squad car and saw the dirt road ahead to the left.

"There it is," he whispered, activating his turn signal. He gently turned onto the dirt road and began following it into the valley.

The squad car's headlights popped on, and the cruiser rolled after them.

"Oh crap," said Jaelyn. "He's following us."

Donnie was mortified. His hands gripped the steering wheel tightly, desperately. "He doesn't have his siren or flashing lights on," he noted.

"Maybe he just wants to see where we're going," said

Jaelyn. "To make sure we're not up to causing trouble for the Amish."

"We can't stop now," Donnie stated. "All we have to do is make it to the Amish community. After that—as long as what Greg told me was true—the Amish can tell the cops that we're expected and send them away."

The road was lumpy with small rock protrusions, clumps of prairie grass, and rain ruts. Donnie maintained a slow pace and stared ahead. He soon saw a cluster of houses in the distance. *Almost there*, he told himself, praying the police would not try to stop him.

By the time the van arrived at the community, three men were standing at the end of the road to meet them. The light from the lanterns they were holding showed their faces. The men had graying beards, mindful eyes, and tight scowls.

Donnie shut off the engine. "Stay here," he told Jaelyn, "and make sure Lance doesn't wake up or move around." Then he opened the door and stepped out of the van. "Hello, sirs," he said, greeting the landowners. "My name is Donnie Bowser, and my friend Greg Thomson told me you would be expecting me."

He heard a car door shut behind him as a policeman exited the cruiser.

Donnie kept his eyes on the stiff Amish. "I've brought my brother, who is possessed by a bad spirit. Please tell me it's okay that we came."

The eldest of the three stepped forward. Donnie thought for sure that this was a huge mistake, that the Amish would deem him a trespasser, and that the police would arrest him.

"Yes, young man, we've been expecting you." The

man's eyes then wandered past Donnie and to the policeman behind him. "We all have."

Donnie turned to address the officer. A middle-aged man with a neat mustache was approaching, the badge on his uniform shimmering in the light from the lanterns. His eyes were friendly, reassuring, and there was a smile on his face.

"Hello, Donnie," the lawman said. "I'm Sheriff Skelton. Your friends informed me of the situation, and I reached out to these good people on their behalf."

Donnie was stunned. "Wait, you mean you know why we're here?"

"Some sort of exorcism," the sheriff confirmed. "I'll be honest, I wasn't sure what to make of the story when I heard it, but then some pieces came together for me, and I knew I had to help."

"What pieces came together?" asked Donnie, curious.

"Well, like the mention of Jack Grainger, for one. And the chest that your friends brought out of the field. There has always been a legend about a witch that imprisoned his soul in a wooden box. Now it would seem there might be some truth to that. And I have an unsolved murder on my hands that seems to be related."

Donnie's pulse was still quick. "My brother didn't kill anybody. And I'm sure none of his friends did either."

"We don't believe he did," said the Amish elder. "If an evil is inside him, then your brother is nothing more than an innocent victim."

Donnie felt a wave of relief flow through him. "Thank God," he breathed.

"I am Jacob," the man stated. "These are my brothers,

David and Isaiah." He looked at the van. "Is he in there?"

"Yes," said Donnie. He signaled for Jaelyn to come out, and she did.

"Let us take him to the barn. He must be prepared there."

Donnie brought the group to the side of the van. Then he opened the door and climbed inside. The sheriff followed, illuminating the interior with his flashlight. Lance was lying on the cushions in the back, still knocked out. Donnie and the sheriff took hold of the skinny man and carried him out of the vehicle.

Jacob led the group to the community barn. It was a sizable structure, with double sliding doors covering its entrance. Jacob rolled one of the doors aside and went inside to light more lanterns.

Donnie studied the barn's interior while they walked. Off to the right was a stabling area, where half a dozen horses were put up. Several wagons were parked on the left, one propped on a stand while in the middle of a repair.

"Bring him here," said Jacob, standing next to a barrel that had been placed against a post. Donnie and the sheriff seated Lance atop the barrel. "Hold him up." Jacob wrapped a rope around Lance's chest and bound him to the lumber post. Then he secured Lance's wrists together with cloth.

Jaelyn drew nearer to examine Lance. He was still unconscious. She checked his breathing and his pulse; both were unlabored. She kissed his forehead and turned to address Donnie. "Should I give him another dose?"

"I think that'd be okay," said Donnie. "It's been a while since the last one."

"Okay." Jaelyn rushed to the van, pulled another syringe from her suitcase, and returned to the barn. She administered the dose into Lance's arm. "Hopefully, this will keep him asleep through the night." She waited a minute or two, checked his pulse once more, and kissed his forehead again.

Jacob stood before the restrained young man and bowed his head. He uttered some type of prayer spoken in what sounded like German. Then he turned to his guests. "Come now," he offered, "let us go inside the house."

The elder led the others out of the barn. He rolled the door shut, brought the group to his house, and ushered them inside.

Jaelyn studied the quaint home when she entered. There were coats and straw hats hanging on the wall, hearty furniture crafted from oak, a propane lamp, a wood-burning stove, and hand-stitched quilts stacked in the corner. In the kitchen was an indoor garden yielding beans and peas, and the shelves were packed with canned vegetables and fruits. It was obvious this was a community of farmers.

"Please, be seated," said Jacob.

Donnie, Jaelyn, and the sheriff pulled chairs from the dining table and sat down. Jacob sat at the head of the table while his brothers stood in the background. Donnie took note of their appearance; the Amish looked exactly as he imagined they would. Facial hair spanned the perimeters of their jaws and chins, although they were neatly shaved around their lips, and they wore homespun clothing with suspenders.

"Are you hungry?" the host enquired. "I can have Ruth prepare some food for you."

"Oh no, thank you," Donnie replied politely. "It's much too late."

"So," said Jacob, folding his hands. "Tell me about the spirit in your brother. I need to know everything."

"Well," Donnie began, "we believe it is a killer named Jack Grainger, who died in this town a long time ago."

"1882," Sheriff Skelton added. "When apparently a woman practicing black magic killed him for murdering her brother."

Donnie nodded. "A voodoo priestess and she somehow found and killed Grainger."

"And burned his body," the sheriff enlightened. "His ashes are allegedly what she buried in that chest."

"And we dug it up...," Jaelyn muttered regretfully. Her eyes were fixed on the chest for a moment, and then she looked at Jacob. "When we first opened it, a hundred cockroaches came out. Our friend Karen said they were palmetto bugs, which live in the South. Just like where the voodoo woman was from. If she cursed his soul to this chest, the bugs might be an element of her curse."

"This was a bad man, Jacob," said Sheriff Skelton. "He tortured and killed many innocent people — including Indian women and children — over the span of about ten years."

Jacob understood. "He is a very angry spirit."

"He almost *killed* me this morning," Donnie admitted. "When I told my brother I was bringing him here, he went berserk. And he made my brother so *strong*...you have to make sure to keep Lance tied up tightly."

"I intend to," assured Jacob. The calm of his face made Donnie think the elder had been through this type of thing before.

Jaelyn was gazing at the floor blankly. "I hope Lance will be okay. I don't even want to think about what it must be like going through what he's experiencing."

"Two souls cannot exist in a single body," said Jacob. "Not for long. One will destroy the other and take over. The longer your friend remains in this state, the more likely it is that his soul will perish."

"Then we should get started right away," Donnie remarked.

Jacob shook his head slowly. "No. It is late, and we need rest. We will tend to him in the morning when our bodies and minds are rejuvenated." He leaned forward. "We will need all the strength we can get."

CHAPTER 33
THE RITE

Everyone regrouped in front of the barn the next morning, just after sunup. Sheriff Skelton returned to the property to witness the morning's activities. He emerged from his cruiser to join the others.

Donnie and Jaelyn acknowledged the sheriff as he neared. Jaelyn was holding a small, wooden chest, and the sheriff's eyes were drawn to it. *That must be it*, he figured. *The chest Grainger's soul was buried in.* Standing next to the pair were Jacob, his brothers, and five other men from the community. Jacob gave a subtle wave with one hand while holding his Bible in the other.

"Morning, all," the sheriff said. "I guess it's time to check on our guest." Jacob nodded accordingly.

"All right," said Donnie, "how do we do this?"

"He will remain restrained," Jacob stated. "No matter what he says, he must not be released until we have succeeded."

"Agreed." Donnie remembered the vicious strength Grainger gave Lance, and he understood the need to keep everybody safe.

"This must be done in the presence of ten men. With you and the good sheriff, we have ten." Jacob glanced at Jaelyn with uncertainty. Having a woman there was not their way.

Jaelyn sensed what Jacob was uncomfortable about. "Don't worry about me," she assured. "I'll stand behind everyone and stay out of the way."

Jacob nodded. "All right." He placed his hand on one of the barn doors, gripping the edge. "Remember," he said, "the spirit inside this young man is very dark. He may be very difficult to cast out. But we must not give up until it is done." Then he pulled the door open, letting the morning light into the barn.

Lance was awake. His eyes were wild, confused, scared. They widened upon seeing Donnie and Jaelyn.

"What am I doing here?" he asked through cracked lips.

"You are here to be healed," said Jacob, stepping up to the man in custody.

Lance wriggled uncomfortably on the barrel. He looked extremely dehydrated. "I'm thirsty."

Jacob stepped back and motioned for Donnie to give his brother water. Donnie brought his water bottle to Lance's parched lips and slowly poured it into his mouth. Lance gulped it down eagerly. Then he brought his feeble gaze up to his brother.

"Why are you doing this to me?"

"You know why," Donnie said softly.

"That's enough; it is time to begin." Jacob approached Lance. He flung blessed salt and water upon his subject. "Remain calm and still, in the name of Jesus Christ," Jacob commanded. Then he opened his Bible, laid his right hand on Lance's head, and began reading a prayer.

"In the name of Jesus, Jesus, Jesus, that which cannot abide, depart. In the name of Jesus, Jesus, Jesus, that which cannot abide, depart. In the name of Jesus, Jesus, Jesus, that which cannot abide, depart."

Jacob paused, then delivered the next part of the prayer.

"In the name of Yeshuah, Yeshuah, Yeshuah, that which cannot abide depart. In the name of Yeshuah, Yeshuah, Yeshuah, that which cannot abide depart. In the name of Yeshuah, Yeshuah, Yeshuah, that which cannot abide depart."

Another pause.

"In the name of Yehoshuah, Yehoshuah, Yehoshuah, that which cannot abide depart. In the name of Yehoshuah, Yehoshuah, Yehoshuah, that which cannot abide depart. In the name of Yehoshuah, Yehoshuah, Yehoshuah, that which cannot abide depart." Then, "Amen, Amen, Amen."

Lance's head slowly rose. His eyes were dark. They looked black in the dim light of the barn.

Jaelyn felt a chill dribble down her spine. Those were the same eyes she'd seen in his apartment when he became violent.

A gritty voice escaped his lips. "I don't obey your God."

"Who are you?" asked Jacob.

"Am I not Lance Bowser?"

"You are not Lance Bowser. You are Jack Grainger."

Lance's head tilted, and a sinful smile appeared. "In the flesh."

Diligent in his task, the elder continued his prayers. The holy words were clearly annoying the spirit of Grainger, but they did not compel him to leave Lance's body. Grainger wriggled harder as he grew more irritated. But the knotted cloth would not release its grip on Lance's wrists.

More prayers from Jacob. Then commands demanding the spirit's departure, accompaniment by his brothers, also calling for Grainger's expulsion.

Lance's eyes went directly to Donnie. "Is this what you wanted? To hurt him? Do you feel like a big man torturing your little brother? Your poor, harmless brother?"

You're anything but harmless, Donnie reminded himself.

"Is this how you get even with Daddy? What would Daddy think of you now?"

Donnie brushed off the attempt to upset him. He knew the spirit of Grainger was swimming inside his brother's mind, and it would try to use anything it found there as a weapon. Donnie would not be thrown.

"You only see what you interpret from my brother's memories," Donnie said with a calm smile. "You don't know the *truth* about anything, Grainger. It's sad that you think you can use that against me." He stepped closer to Lance. "I don't have a daddy. I have a brother. And I will see you back to the grave to get him back."

"Blah, blah, blah," the voice groaned. "You are nothing. Just like your father believes."

Jacob rested his hand on Donnie's shoulder and gently pulled him back. There was no time for further distractions.

A scowl hardened on Lance's face as the spirit returned his gaze to Jacob. "And as for you cocksuckers—"

"Be silent!" bellowed Jacob. "In the name of Jesus, I command you to leave the body of this man!" He sprinkled more salt and water over Lance.

"I'll kill you all!" Lance's body convulsed violently, attempting to break free from its restraints. "I'll skin you, bleed you out! And your families too! Lousy cocksuckers!"

Donnie watched the cloth bindings closely, praying the knots would not loosen. They held, despite being yanked so viciously. Donnie figured Lance's wrists were probably bruising pretty badly.

"And you, missy," said Grainger, looking at Jaelyn. "You couldn't even carry a child."

She was shaken to the core. "Wh…?"

"You let it die inside you. Now you're going to watch these men murder your boyfriend? You're worthless."

Her face showed she was hurt deeply by the verbal onslaught.

Jacob knew what Grainger was doing, and he had to put a stop to the divisive distractions. "Silence!" Jacob ordered. "In the name of Jesus, foul spirit, leave this body now!"

"You are not a priest!"

"Nay, yet I am a servant of God, and His power is with me this day."

Grainger chortled. "We'll see."

Jacob continued reading from the Bible. The process was long, with many phrases being repeated over and over again. Then Jacob began reciting prayers in a German dialect. He grew more passionate and animated as he went.

But still, Grainger did not break.

"Heh heh heh," he chuckled. "Too bad I don't speak whatever language that is."

"In the name of God, depart from this body!" demanded Jacob.

"I already told you," Grainger growled, "I don't believe in your God."

But Lance does, thought Jaelyn.

She knew her boyfriend, inside and out, and that he could be strong when he needed to. She supported and respected his recent discovery of faith. His desire to find a path to God was admirable, even if it was not something she believed in. Maybe Lance needed some of that faith now.

"Ask God to help you, Lance!" she blurted, and the men in the barn turned to look at her. She ignored their stares and continued. "You believe in God, and He believes in you! Use your faith and fight! He will fight with you, Lance. If you believe, you will succeed."

Lance's body was still for a moment. Then Grainger began to struggle. Lance's muscles twitched and contracted all over his body. It looked like two cats were scrapping inside a burlap sack.

It seemed to be working.

"*Fight* him, Lance!" Jaelyn fueled. "Force him out! God will give you the strength to expel him!"

The body was convulsing rapidly now. Lance's mouth opened, and something brown could be seen moving inside.

It was a palmetto bug.

Aware of the connection between the Southern insects and the chest they belonged to, Jaelyn rushed forward and placed the wooden chest on the ground in front of Lance. She removed the lid and stepped back. The bug reluctantly emerged from Lance's mouth.

Jacob understood what she was doing. Having remembered everything they told him last night, he decided he would assist with this approach. Grainger did not seem to comply in God's name, but perhaps he would obey in the name of the voodoo woman who cursed him.

"In the name of she who owns your soul, return to the place you are condemned to!"

Lance grimaced, clearly in pain.

Jacob's voice grew louder, stronger. "Return to your resting place! Your master commands it! She who owns your soul!"

"Come on, Lance!" said Jaelyn. "Use your faith!"

Lance's head fell back, and Grainger's voice roared, bellowed, screamed up to the rafters. Then the vocal outburst became muffled. Reddish-brown insects rose from Lance's throat and began to gush from his mouth.

Donnie's eyes were wide. "Holy shit...," he burbled, taking in the unbelievable sight. It was a nightmarish image he would never forget.

The palmetto bugs flowed in a direct line down Lance's body and toward the open chest. They obediently scuttled into the wooden box and packed themselves inside. Jacob and his brothers were terrified, but they stayed where they were and watched in awe.

By the time the last insect left Lance's mouth, the count must have been near a hundred bugs. The last of the palmetto bugs journeyed across the floor and into their wooden home.

Jaelyn quickly placed the lid on top, and Donnie rushed over to strap it shut.

A silence fell over the barn.

Everybody in the room scanned each other's eyes, assuring themselves that they were not the only ones who saw what they thought they had just seen. Lance's head was drooped in exhaustion, his eyes closed. Donnie crept up to his brother and placed his hands on Lance's shoulders.

"Open your eyes, Lance," said Donnie. The sight of Lance so weak, weary, and beaten crushed his heart. Donnie held back tears that longed to pour out for his brother. He had to stay strong. "Open your eyes, little brother."

Lance's eyes fluttered open. They were glossy. He blinked and looked around to study his surroundings. He smiled up at Donnie. Lance tried to speak but could only mouth his big brother's name with reverence.

CHAPTER 34
GHOSTFIELD

The van rolled past the church. Lance and Jaelyn looked at the white structure, their eyes softening at the familiar sight. There was something comforting about seeing it again.

"Keep going?" Donnie asked.

"Keep going," said Lance. "The road veers left up ahead, then right again." His voice was still raspy from having strained vocal cords, but it was getting better.

Donnie navigated the dirt road as directed. He took it slow when it became bumpy, not wanting to jostle his passengers any. Or their cargo.

He had picked up some supplies at the local hardware store. Shovels, a pick, a 2x4 stud, a five-gallon bucket, bags of concrete, and a dozen gallons of water. He had also picked up a tie-down, which he used to strap the wooden chest securely shut.

The road ended half a mile from the church. Lance surveyed the field around them. "Yeah, this is it. We walked from here, that way." He pointed in a specific direction.

Donnie shut off the engine. "Let's go check it out."

The trio exited the van and began walking into the field. Recalling the trail the students took the night they followed the ghost lights into the darkness, Lance and Jaelyn wandered the same path through the sagebrush and field grass. Spotting the same gravesite they had seen before confirmed that they were going the right way.

"I remember these," said Jaelyn.

Donnie glanced at the few graves with small, wooden crosses reaching up from the ground. "No names," he noted.

"It's just a little farther," said Lance. "This way, I think."

Five minutes later, Lance spotted the earthen pit they were seeking. He recognized the crater-like depression in the ground. A smirk — of both smugness and humility — stretched his face. "This is it," he sighed.

Donnie placed his hands on his hips. The pit was eight feet wide, not terribly deep, and had a small hole in the bottom. He figured that was where the chest used to reside.

"And that's where the box has to go back to," said Donnie. "That exact spot, actually, in case the voodoo woman blessed or cursed, or whatever, that area. I trust that whatever she did the first time was enough to keep the spirit contained here." He turned to face his brother. "And the concrete we're gonna add will ensure that."

"Yes." Lance was all for sealing that chest so that it could never be opened again.

"So, we'll start by digging a bigger hole around that spot. Then we'll pour some concrete in, set the soul box in the center, and pour more concrete to cover the top. The box will be completely encased, secure forever."

Jaelyn was satisfied with the plan. "Perfect," she said.

"Come on," said Donnie, "let's go get the stuff from the van." He led the others back to the brown van.

He opened the side door and began pulling their supplies out. He grabbed two of the shovels and handed them to his partners. Seeing the bruises on Lance's wrists, Donnie still felt bad about having him bound. But he forgave himself, knowing it was the only option. Temporary bruising was a small price to pay for his brother to be back.

The group hauled their digging tools to the pit. They carefully slid down the sloped embankment and reached the bottom. Lance slowly stepped closer to the spot where he had discovered the buried chest. He swallowed down the emotions swirling inside him.

"Here we go," stated Donnie. He thrust his shovel into the dry earth around the hole and began carving a larger tomb. Lance and Jaelyn followed his example and dug a three-foot-wide perimeter. Occasionally they were met with stubborn rocks, which Donnie removed with the pick.

Before long, the new grave was over two feet deep. Donnie stepped back. "You two keep going," he said, "while I start mixing the concrete."

"Okay," said Jaelyn. "How deep do we need to dig?"

Lance looked at his brother, who simply shrugged. Then, trying to suppress the horrible memories of recent events, he said, "As deep as we can."

Michael Yowell is an American horror writer residing in South Carolina. His published works include the short story collection *Fragments And Shards*, his serial-killer-vs-reporter novel *The Camera Eye*, the werewolf hunter books *The Dogcatcher*, *The Dogcatcher II: Chupacabras*, and *The Dogcatcher III: Werewolf Queen*, his wild sea monsters trilogy *Sliggers*, *Sligger Island*, and *Sligger Invasion*, and the creepy chiller *Ghostfield*. And don't forget his Western (yes, Western!) *Red Pines*.

www.ingramcontent.com/pod-product-compliance
Lightning Source LLC
Chambersburg PA
CBHW030137180626
46812CB00002B/724